# MÈO AND BÉ

## DOAN PHUONG NGUYEN

**Tu Books**

*An imprint of* LEE & LOW BOOKS INC.

New York

TU BOOKS, *an imprint of* LEE & LOW BOOKS INC.
95 Madison Avenue, New York, NY 10016
leeandlow.com

Manufactured in the United States of America
Printed on paper from responsible sources

Edited by Elise McMullen-Ciotti
Book design by Sheila Smallwood
Typesetting by ElfElm Publishing
Book production by The Kids at Our House
The text is set in Adobe Text Pro
The illustrations are rendered in Procreate and Adobe Photoshop

10 9 8 7 6 5 4 3 2 1
First Edition

Library of Congress Cataloging-in-Publication Data
Names: Nguyen, DoanPhuong, author.
Title: Mèo and Bé / DoanPhuong Nguyen.
Description: First edition. | New York : Tu Books, an imprint of Lee & Low Books Inc.,
   [2023] | Audience: Ages 10-14. | Summary: In 1964, before the United States enters the
   Vietnam War, eleven-year-old Bé and her three-footed kitten Mèo must rise above a
   broken home and the injustices of war to find the comfort, safety, and love of a found
   family.
Identifiers: LCCN 2022045011 | ISBN 9781643796253 (hardcover) |
   ISBN 9781643796260 (ebk)
Subjects: LCSH: Vietnam War,1961-1975—Juvenile fiction. | CYAC: Vietnam War,1961–
   1975—Fiction. | Vietnam—History—1945-1975—Fiction. | Mutism—Fiction. | Human-
   animal relationships—Fiction. | Human trafficking—Fiction. | Survival—Fiction. |
   LCGFT: Historical fiction. | Novels.
Classification: LCC PZ7.1.N517 Me 2023 | DDC [Fic]—dc23
LC record available at https://lccn.loc.gov/2022045011

*For my parents, Hoang and Mỹ Dung, whose sacrifices enabled me to grow up and have a more prosperous future, and to the memory of Miss Helen and Pat, who nurtured my love of reading and books. To Joshua, for always supporting my crazy ideas, and to Luke, I hope you always chase after your dreams.*

# A NOTE TO READERS

*Mèo and Bé* takes place in Vietnam in the 1960s, and there are many Vietnamese names and words throughout the story. If you'd like to try and sound these words out as you read, here is a pronunciation guide and a glossary for your reference. In the glossary's sound spellings:

"a" sounds like "cat"

"ai" sounds like "eye"

"e" sounds like "let"

"ee" sounds like "feet"

"ew" sounds like "few"

"i" sounds like "sit"

"o" sounds like "more"

"ow" sounds like "ouch"

"oy" sounds like "boy"

"ock" sounds like "sock"

Cảm ơn bạn đã đọc! (Thank you for reading!)

# VIETNAMESE NAMES

**Bà Già** (ba ya)

**Bảo** (bow)

**Bé** (beah)

**Cha** (tcha)

**Chi Yen** (chee eeng)

**Chú Cuội** (choo gwuh-oy)

**Cô Bích** (goh bick)

**Cô Huệ** (goh hwe)

**Cô Lan** (goh lahng)

**Cô Nga** (goh ngah)

**Đoan Phương** (dwahng fuhng)

**Hiếu** (heew)

**Hoàng** (hwahng)

**Mai An Tiêm** (my ahng tee-uhm)

**Mê Kông** (mee kohng)

**Mèo** (me-ow)

**Mỹ Dung** (mee yuhng)

**Ngân** (nguhng)

**Ngô Đinh Diệm** (ngoh dihn yee-uhm)

**Nhật** (nee-at)

**Ông Đình** (ohm din)

**Sang** (shang)

**Thương** (tuh-uhng)

**Trân** (tran)

**Tuyết** (tway-et)

**Út** (uhdt)

**Văn** (vahn)

**Xuân** (swuhng)

# VIETNAMESE GLOSSARY

**áo bà ba** (ow ba ba): a traditional South Vietnamese garment

**áo dài** (ow yai): Vietnamese national dress

**Ba** (ba): Father

**Bà Nội** (ba noh-ih): Paternal Grandmother

**bánh bao** (bahn bow): a steamed bun, most often stuffed with pork and egg

**bánh chưng** (bahn truhng): Vietnamese sticky rice cake, traditionally eaten at Tết

**bánh mì** (bahn mee): a Vietnamese sandwich, traditionally stuffed with meat and pickled vegetables

**cà phê sữa đá** (kah feh shuh dah): Vietnamese iced coffee

**chả giò** (tcha ja): fried egg roll

**cháo** (chow-ow): rice porridge

**chè** (chee-eh): a type of Vietnamese dessert

**chợ chồm hổm** (choh chom hom): a street market where the women squat to sell their produce

**Cô** (goh): Auntie, Aunt, or a polite term for an unmarried girl

**con** (gong): child

**con khỉ** (gong kee): monkeys

**con quay** (gong gwai): spinning tops

**Đồi Khỉ** (dowih kee): Monkey Hill

**gỏi cuốn** (goy gwuhng): Vietnamese spring rolls

**khai sinh** (kai shin): birth certificate

**lì xì** (lee see): lucky New Year's money

**Má** (ma): Mother

**múa lân** (mwhuh luhng) : unicorn dance, usually performed during the New Year

**nước mía** (noo-ock mee-ah): sugarcane juice

**Ông Địa** (ong deeuh): Spirit of the Earth

**Tết** (teht): Vietnamese New Year

**Việt Cộng** (vee-et cahm): Vietnamese Communists

**xe đò** (seh do): a bus for long-distance travel; a passenger bus

**xích lô** (sit loh): a three-wheeled pedicab

# PART 1
# SUNSHINE AND PADDY SNAILS

# CHAPTER 1

Tʜưᴏɴɢ's sᴀɴᴅᴀʟs kicked up dust from the dirt road, caking her white school uniform in a light layer of brown grime. Má had said it was good for Thương to have strong leg muscles, because with them, she could outrun anything. Thương hoped she would never have to outrun the scary Việt Cộng—the communist guerilla forces who had been waging war against the South for longer than she'd been alive. Yet, as the days passed, the war loomed closer, like an ominous cloud gathering before a storm.

She ran to the coffee shop where Má worked, waving to two South Vietnamese soldiers who patrolled her village. She wasn't afraid of the soldiers or the guns they carried. Everyone knew that the Việt Cộng hid in the mountains, and she lived in the lowlands where it was still safe. For now.

But that day, April 13, 1962, Thương wasn't thinking about the war. Excitement bubbled up inside her as she thought of Ba, who was coming home for his monthly visit, and she couldn't wait to see what toys and gifts her father would bring this time.

The coffee shop was busy with patrons drinking cà phê sữa đá—Vietnamese iced coffee—smoking cigarettes, and reading newspapers as they chatted about the war and President Ngô Đinh Diệm. Má was in the back, pouring boiling water into a row of stainless steel phin filters over coffee glasses. She wore a light pink áo dài, and her long black hair was pulled back into a ponytail.

Ba wasn't anywhere in sight.

"When is he coming, Má? Why isn't he here yet?" Thương asked.

"It is getting more dangerous to travel," Má said with a deep sigh, worry lines dotting her forehead. "He'll be here soon."

"Why can't he just come to live with us, where it's not dangerous?" Thương said, watching the droplets of coffee trickle into the glasses.

"It's not as easy as that. He has land farther north. He can't abandon his property. It's better this way," she said.

"But why?" Thương asked.

Now that Thương was nine, she wanted to know more about Ba's life elsewhere, but Má always avoided her questions.

"Go, take these coffees to that table in the front, and then you can wait for your father at the empty table next to them."

Thương did as she was asked and then sat waiting impatiently for Ba to arrive. She wished she could be with Ba always, instead of only one weekend a month.

Thankfully, she didn't have to wait long before she saw his motorbike turning a corner in the distance. She jumped up and ran down the street toward him. He slowed and stopped when he saw her.

"Ba! I have so much to tell you! Our neighbor Cô Nga, her cat—you know the one that ate Ông Đình's bird—she had kittens! But then she gave them all away, and Má said I couldn't have one. Can you convince her to let me have one? Please?" Thương said, talking a kilometer a minute.

"Slow down. You can tell me all about it later. Hop on. Let's go see your mother. I've missed you both very much," Ba said.

Thương grabbed onto Ba's muscular arm, climbed up, and hugged him from behind. He smelled of cigarette smoke and warmth, and she loved how cozy she felt as she pressed her cheek against his shoulder. Although he was older than Má by more than a decade, he didn't have the air of an older man. He was strong and youthful, with hard abs and a brawny frame.

The motorbike roared back to life and Thương smiled, the wind whipping her waist-length black hair behind her, as they drove the short distance to the coffee shop.

Má's face brightened when she saw Ba, relief flooding her features. He sat down at a table near the back, and she prepared him a glass of coffee. She placed her hand on his shoulder as she left the cup, and he squeezed it before she went back to her work.

Thương sat at the table across from Ba, watching as he opened up his satchel and unfolded a colorful kite shaped like a phoenix. Her eyes lit up, and she bounced up and down.

"Tomorrow, we can fly it . . . and there's more." Ba brought out a little bamboo boat and a small drum on a stick that had two pellets hanging on strings.

Thương jumped up and flung her arms around his neck and squeezed. "Thank you, Ba!" Ba laughed. She grabbed the drum, rubbed its stick between her hands, and watched the pellets hit the head of the drum, making a rattling noise. It was fun, but too noisy for the coffee shop.

"Can I go to Sang's house while Má closes the shop? I want to show her my toys."

"Go. We'll see you within the hour," Má said.

Thương grabbed the bamboo boat and drum and ran down the road to visit her best friend.

When her parents arrived to collect her an hour later, Sang was playing with the toy drum while Thương was petting Cô Nga's cat, who had wandered into the yard. They looked like sisters playing together, still wearing their school uniforms. The only difference was that Sang had shoulder-length black hair.

The girls giggled as Thương sang a made-up tune to the beat of the drum. *"Mew, mew, mew, the cat likes me. No, no, no, the cat loves me."*

"These gifts are much better than the ones your Ba brought you last month," Sang said.

"No, they aren't. I loved those edible figurines, especially the princess," Thương said.

"But then we ate them." Sang giggled. "They were yummy. Tell him to buy you more next month."

"Time to go," Má called from Sang's courtyard.

Thương gave the cat a last head rub and jumped up. She waved to her friend and joined her parents.

"I wish you'd let me have a kitten," Thương complained as they walked across the street to the one-room house where she and Má lived.

For dinner, the family ate rice with fried fish and water spinach soup, and they had fresh vú sữa—star apple—for dessert. Má cut the fruit in half, and Thương used a spoon to scoop out the flesh and eat it, its milky sweet juice dripping down her chin.

Ba then handed a small red box to Má. "I brought

you something too, my love. You didn't think I'd come without a gift, did you?"

Má smiled and gazed affectionately at Ba. Thương had to look away because it was too mushy. Má opened the box to find a beautiful jade bracelet. As her parents held hands and silently gazed at each other, Thương examined the bracelet, looping it onto her too-small wrists. It was smooth and felt nice against her skin, and it was the prettiest green color.

Later, the three of them snuggled together in bed. Thương lay in the middle, feeling content and cozy while Ba began recounting the legend of Mai An Tiêm—how watermelons were brought to Vietnam. Má waved a paper fan over her, cooling her. The air was hot and stuffy in the room, and it would only get hotter when summer came.

"Mai An Tiêm was the king's adopted son," Ba began. "He and his family were lavished with many luxuries and gifts, but he was ungrateful. One day, he angered the king so badly that the king banished him, his wife, and his children to live on a deserted island in the middle of the ocean."

"Oh no! How did they survive?" Thương asked.

"They looked for food on the island. Finally, Mai An Tiêm came across birds eating a red-fleshed fruit with black seeds. He thought, if the birds can eat that, so can I. So Mai An Tiêm planted the seeds and the fruit grew. When they were ripe, he and his family enjoyed the most delicious watermelon."

"How did they get off the island?" Thương asked with a yawn.

"Mai An Tiêm carved his name on a watermelon he grew, and he sent it off floating into the sea, hoping sailors would find it and stop to exchange food and rice with his family. It worked. Soon, his watermelons were very popular with sailors, who came to the island to trade rice for the delicious fruit. It wasn't long before the king had his first taste of watermelon and discovered it was grown by his son on the island . . . "

Thương smiled, drifting off to sleep in the middle of the story, happy and secure with both her parents beside her.

Later in the night, she woke with a start to angry whispers coming from the other side of the room. Her parents were huddled together, fighting. Thương had never seen them argue before. She leaned on her elbows and strained to hear what they were saying.

"No. That is the worst idea. I will not do it. I refuse. Are you crazy? She will murder me!" Má's voice rose to a shout. "You have to think of Thương!"

"I am. It is the only way we can be together. The war is only getting worse. President Diệm survived an assassination attempt in February. The Việt Cộng numbers are growing here in the South, and the Americans are becoming more involved in the war," Ba said.

"This village is the safest place for Thương and me. There are no Việt Cộng nearby. You live near the mountains, where they have their strongholds. It's only a matter of time before . . . ," Má said.

"Eventually, they will come here too," Ba said.

"No. It is safest for us to stay here," Má said with a deep sigh.

"I risk my life each time to come down to you, and it is a long journey. It will be safest if we are all together with my family."

Thương was confused. *His family? What is Ba talking about?*

"We are your family too," Má said.

"And I don't want to give you up, so this is the only way. When you come, no one in my home will dare defy my wishes. You will be safe," Ba said.

Má turned to see Thương awake and rushed over. "Go back to sleep."

"Why are you fighting?" Thương asked.

"It is nothing," Má said, picking up the fan and getting back into the bed. She smoothed her daughter's hair and began fanning once more. "Go to sleep now. Ba will show you how to fly a kite tomorrow. Won't that be exciting?"

Thương nodded and closed her eyes, but she had a sinking feeling something very bad was about to happen.

## CHAPTER 2

THE NEXT MORNING, after breakfast, the family headed to the stream in their neighborhood. Má washed clothes at the edge of the water, while Ba taught Thương how to fly a kite.

"Do you feel the direction the wind blows?" Ba asked, handing Thương the spool of the kite. "Put your back to the wind. Hold the kite up and let the wind catch it."

The breeze blew through her short-sleeved, light-yellow shirt, flipping up the collar and cooling her slightly. Thương watched as Ba launched the kite. It caught the draft and hung in the air. She squealed.

"Now we loosen the string. Ah, there it goes." Ba handed her the spool for her to fly it on her own.

The phoenix kite soared into the air above them, and Thương ran up and down the length of the stream, following the wind and laughing. She loved watching her kite fly, and she wished she could soar above too—like a mythical phoenix.

If she could fly, Thương would go to the beach every day, chase after crabs, and bury Ba in the sand like she'd done once before. She'd eat mangoes dipped in salt from a passing vendor, and she would go swimming until her arms hurt. But the beach was a day's motorbike ride away, too far for them to go very often. It was always a special treat.

When Thương was exhausted from kite flying, the family went to a phở stand for lunch. Thương slurped up the noodles and enjoyed the taste of beef and savory broth. Beef phở was her favorite noodle soup.

"How would you like to see me every day, instead of only once a month?" Ba asked, finishing up his bowl of phở.

"I would love that!" Thương said, smiling, but then she looked over at Má, who was frowning. Thương's smile faltered.

"With the war progressing, it is too dangerous for me to come here every month. I've decided the safest option is for us to be together in one place. Next month, you and your mother will move to my home farther north. I have a big house there with lots of land, chickens, and pigs, and you'll have five older brothers to play with," Ba said.

"Five older brothers?" Thương asked, confused.

"It's time for us to tell you the truth. You are old enough now," Má said. She looked over at Ba with the saddest expression on her face.

Thương's stomach flopped, as she remembered the big fight her parents had had the night before. Did this truth have something to do with that?

Ba was silent for a moment before he spoke. "You already know that I live somewhere else when I am not here."

Thương nodded.

"I have another family. Your mother is my second wife and we married before you were born. But I have another wife, who you will call Big Mother. She and I were arranged to be married by my parents when I was only eighteen. Then I did not have a choice, but I chose your mother, and I chose you."

Thương blinked. "You can have more than one wife?"

"In the old days, you could, but now they've changed the law. We married before things changed," Ba explained. "We will all live together as one big family. You have a grandmother too. She will love you. You are the only girl in our family."

A grandmother, and brothers. And she'd see Ba every day. Thương wanted to be excited, but Má didn't look happy. She had a faraway look in her eyes.

"Má is coming too?" Thương asked, suddenly very nervous about this move.

Her mother nodded. "I won't leave you."

The next weeks were a flurry of packing, choosing what to bring and what to leave behind, and saying good-bye to neighbors and friends. They didn't bring much: mostly clothing, the black-and-white photographs they'd taken as a family, and a couple of special items that Ba had given them over the years. Everything fit neatly into one valise.

The morning they were leaving, Má put on a light yellow áo dài embroidered with cherry blossoms along the side and pulled her hair up into a bun. She slipped on the jade bracelet Ba had gifted her, and a gold necklace he'd given her the month before that. Thương thought her mother was the most beautiful woman who'd ever lived.

Thương bounced with nerves as Má braided her hair.

"We must make a good impression," Má said. "Especially for your Bà Nội."

"Have you ever met my grandmother before?" Thương asked.

"No, but your father says she is a kind and understanding woman." Má tied pretty lace ribbons at the ends of Thương's pigtails. "Now, let's put on this dress, and you'll be ready."

Thương slipped on a collared dress that came down to her knees. It was the same yellow color as her mother's áo dài.

Their neighbors came to the bus stop to see them off.

As Má said her goodbyes, thanking everyone for their help over the years, Thương hugged her best friend.

"Don't forget me," Sang said, with tears in her eyes.

"I won't!" Thương said.

Then Má and Thương boarded a crowded bus, their belongings hoisted on top with everyone else's things, and the bus roared to life, bumping down the road.

Thương waved to everyone from the bus window. Má had that far-off look in her eyes again, and she didn't smile once during their two-hour bus ride to Ba's village. Thương fell asleep to the rhythmic sound of the bus's engine.

# CHAPTER 3

Ba was waiting for them at the bus stop. He greeted Má with a kiss on the cheek and then knelt to hug Thương. After strapping on their valise, the three hopped onto Ba's motorbike and drove down the dirt roads to their new home.

Ba's village was located in a more mountainous area of the central highlands in South Vietnam, not too far from the Cambodian border. It was bustling with lots of people, bicycles, motorbikes, buses. The buildings and shops on the side of the road were taller and larger than what she was used to. The road was dusty, and every-thing felt overwhelming to Thương. Her village in the plains had felt safer.

A troop of South Vietnamese soldiers patrolled the streets, and the mountains in the distance made Thương's arm prickle with goosebumps. *Are the Việt Cộng hiding in the mountains right now?* she wondered.

Ba turned the motorbike onto a side street that was less busy than the main road, but it was still full of people. Only a few soldiers patrolled there. Women wearing conical hats carried baskets of produce, balancing them with a bamboo pole on their shoulders. People rode bicycles with huge bundles tied behind them. One man's bicycle was loaded with a massive cage of ducks with their heads poking out, while another man's bike carried a tall stack of bananas.

Houses dotted both sides of the street, their yards protected by fencing. When they approached a wire-fenced yard, Ba made a left onto a long dirt path past a tamarind tree that sat guard at the entrance. The path was dotted with coconut trees that grew low and were laden with young fruit. Out along the edges of the property, Thương saw untamed trees that grew wild and protected the house from the prying eyes of street goers.

Past the grove of coconut trees, there was a vegetable

and herb garden and several empty plots of land. She heard the loud oinking of pigs and looked in the direction of the noise to find a brick-enclosed pigsty. Thương remembered Ba telling her all about how he had come to own his property.

Ba's great-grandfather had been a mandarin, a talented scholar, and an officer in the imperial court who owned many acres of land. After the emperor abdicated in 1945 and the Việt Cộng came to power in the North, the family fell on harder times, but they were far from destitute. *Ba's property is large and lush*, Thương thought.

The motorbike finally came to a stop by a tiled outdoor terrace, which stood in front of a long one-story house with a red, clay-tiled roof. Wing houses with yellow concrete walls were attached on both sides. The wing houses were double the size of the house Thương had shared with Má and looked much newer and less faded than the main house.

*They must be where the bedrooms are*, Thương thought.

A rotund woman with a potbelly stood on the

terrace, her arms crossed, a scowl on her face. She was balding and her face was marred with wrinkles. She looked older than Ba.

The woman looked angry, like a leopard before it jumps on its prey. Thương's stomach flip-flopped. She wanted to hide, but Má grabbed her hand and said, "Be brave."

"That is your Big Mother," Ba said.

Thương didn't want to go up to the terrace. Big Mother looked mean. But Ba took Thương's other hand, and they all walked the two steps up to the terrace together.

"So this is what you've been doing when you disappear every month. I was young once too, had her figure," Big Mother said, her voice strained, fracturing for a split second. Then the sound of hurt was gone, replaced by rage. She sneered, examining Má like a pig to be sold to the butcher.

Thương squeezed Má's hand. She didn't like this woman.

"He'll leave you, too, when you're older and he has no use for you. Once a concubine, always a concubine."

"You will treat her with respect," Ba boomed, his voice commanding. Thương had never heard her father speak so harshly before.

Big Mother grunted.

Thương wanted to ask what a concubine was, but then Big Mother looked at Thương and said, "This little devil looks just like her."

"Don't call her that!" Má snapped. "Of course, she looks like me. She's my daughter."

"She has your nose," Big Mother said bitingly, pointing at Ba.

Thương touched her nose, which was wider and flatter than Má's, and she looked down at her feet. It was the only part of her that was different from Má's. They had the same slender, oval face; the same high cheekbones; a similar arch in their eyebrows; and the same pointed chin.

"You will treat my daughter with the same tenderness you give our children," Ba ordered.

Big Mother crossed her arms.

"Where are the children, anyway?" Ba asked.

"Around here somewhere," Big Mother said. Then,

in an ear-splitting voice, she yelled out, "Bảo, Trân, Nhật, Văn, Xuân, come here *now*!"

Just then, a short elderly woman with heavily freckled skin came out of the main house, leaning heavily on a cane, followed by a group of five boys. She was hunched, her gray hair tied in a neat bun at the top of her head, and she wore a dark purple áo bà ba—a collarless long-sleeved shirt that split at the hips, and matching pants. The boys wore button-down house shirts and pants, and looked like they'd just gotten out of bed, their short hair in disarray.

Thương bowed like Má had instructed her to do. "Hello, Bà Nội. Hello, brothers."

The boys came to stand by their mother, all mumbling "hello." They looked like a mix of Ba and Big Mother. They had Ba's nose, like Thương did, but the shape of their faces and their lips resembled Big Mother's. The youngest boy looked the most like Ba, though he had Big Mother's lips and chin. Every one had a frown on his face and didn't look too friendly, except for the youngest boy, who looked about Thương's age. He smiled and bounced like he couldn't wait to play.

Má narrowed her eyes at the young boy.

Ba introduced the taller boys. "This is Nhật and Văn. They are eighteen and seventeen. Nhật plans to join the South Vietnamese Army soon."

"Me too! Next year, I'm going to fight for our country alongside my brother," Văn said.

Má nodded. "That is very noble of you."

"Trân here is sixteen, Bảo almost thirteen, and—" Ba continued.

"Xuân is ten years old, only a year older than *her,*" Big Mother interjected.

"He's ten?" Má choked, and then she stared at Ba, wide-eyed.

"I'm not the only one who's been betrayed," Big Mother said, smirking for the first time.

Thương didn't understand why Má looked so sad, but then Bà Nội took one of her hands and said, "What is your name, child?" Her skin was as coarse as sand, but she had kind eyes and made Thương feel a little more at ease.

"Thương Thương," the girl replied.

"You named her 'true love?'" Big Mother screamed again.

The older boys made disapproving murmuring sounds. Xuân smiled kindly, not fazed by this at all.

"You selfish, traitorous man," Big Mother said. Her hand moved into the air as if to strike Ba, but he was strong and grabbed her wrist.

Thương winced.

"Don't you dare. This is my house, and my rules. You are to obey me," Ba said.

"She will not be called Thương here. I forbid it," Big Mother spat out.

"That is her name," Má said.

"She is not to be called Thương in my presence. If you must live here, find another name for her," Big Mother said.

Thương shrank back.

"And what do you suggest?" Má said. "Her name is Thương."

"Hmm, why don't we call her Bé?" Bà Nội suggested. "She is the youngest one in our family. The name is fitting. She can be Thương at school and Bé at home."

"Fine," Big Mother said. "But never use her birth name around me."

"Her name is Thương," Má said angrily.

"Let's just call her Bé," Ba said.

"I didn't come here for my daughter's name to be changed," Má said.

"Then you can leave. The exit is right over there," Big Mother said.

"Oh, I would if I could," Má screamed.

The women yelled at one another, and Thương wondered why she and Má couldn't leave. She didn't want her name changed. She'd been Thương her entire life.

"Quiet down!" Ba boomed. "Her name is now Bé. End of argument."

"But I don't want my name changed," Thương protested.

"You don't have a choice, little devil," Big Mother sneered.

Thương—now called Bé—swallowed as she looked up at her scary-looking stepmother. Who was she without her true name?

Xuân pulled his sister toward the yard. "Bé, let's go play! Come on, sister. Follow me!"

Bé wanted to get away. She looked up at Má, silently searching for permission. Má nodded, and Bé ran off with her half-brother.

As Bé chased Xuân through the property, she could hear Má and Big Mother arguing from the terrace, their voices getting more muted the farther she ran from the house.

The siblings ran through the vegetable garden, underneath a bamboo lattice where green luffa gourds were hanging and growing above their heads.

"You're too fast!" Bé huffed.

"Gotta catch me!" Xuân yelled back.

They sprinted past the garden, five empty plots of land, and the pigsty where Bé could hear pigs oinking and making noise.

"Follow me!" Xuân said as he ran into a chicken enclosure at the back of the property and finally stopped.

Bé put her hands on her legs, trying to catch her breath.

Chickens loitered freely around the enclosure, some pecking for food on the ground, while others lay in the hay mound that was as high and wide as a banana tree.

"You have to learn to be fast around here, or my mother will get you. She's mean," Xuân said.

"She looks mean," Bé said quietly.

"Oh, she is. Mostly with me, though. She says I'm the naughtiest." Xuân shrugged. "But when we're back here, we're free. She almost never comes here. I'm the one who collects the eggs, and Ba is the one who kills the chickens when it's time to eat them."

Bé made a face. She knew animals had to be killed for their meat, but she didn't want to see it or know about it.

Bé couldn't help but compare how she looked to Xuân. He was four inches taller, tan—but a shade darker than her—and his face was more round and marred with small scars along his cheekbone. His short hair was big and stuck out in the funniest places. Bé decided he looked friendly, so she asked, "Can I help you collect the eggs?"

"Sure," Xuân said. "They normally lay their eggs in the mound. You have to search to find them."

"Want to see who can collect the most eggs?" Bé asked.

"The winner gets half of the loser's New Year's money," Xuân said. "Let's go!"

They ran to the mound, digging around the hay for eggs. Chickens squawked at them, unhappy with the intrusion. Brother and sister moved fast, pushing hay out of the way in their search. Bé pulled the bottom of her dress up to make a space to put the eggs she found. Xuân used his shirt.

Bé giggled as she raced with her brother, happy for the first time since arriving at her new home.

Bé shifted hay around at the bottom of the mound, but instead of finding an egg, there was a cat with black fur nestled inside. It hissed loudly, claws and teeth out. Bé shrieked and almost dropped her eggs.

"What is it?" Xuân asked, coming to stand by her. "Oh, it's that stray cat again."

"You have a cat?" Bé asked.

"No. My mother says cats are bad luck, especially the black ones. The color of evil, you know? But this one keeps showing up back here. It doesn't bother the chickens, so I just leave it alone."

"I love cats. Here, take my eggs. You win," Bé said,

not even looking to see how many eggs Xuân had collected. Then she sat on the ground and extended her hand slowly. "Here, kitty, kitty, I won't bite."

The black cat cautiously approached and sniffed her hand. It was a scrawny thing with ragged fur and a face that was long and skinny.

"I'm going to name it Bà Già," Bé said. "It looks like an old lady, don't you think?"

"A little," Xuân said, sitting down next to her.

The cat rubbed its head against Bé's hand and purred.

She and Xuân stayed in the chicken enclosure for a long time, playing with Bà Già and collecting eggs. By the time Má came to find Bé, it was almost dinnertime.

"I'll race you!" Xuân said.

And off they went, laughing as they ran back toward the house.

# CHAPTER 4

"**W**HERE HAVE YOU BEEN? Playing with that devil?!" Big Mother's voice boomed from the outdoor kitchen. Xuân and Bé stopped running, hanging back on the terrace. Bé's heart pounded as she waited for Má to catch up to them. Big Mother came out and pulled Xuân by the collar of his shirt. He stumbled. "Do not go near her."

"I told you not to call her that," Má said, her voice seething. "We agreed on Bé."

"When *my* husband and mother-in-law aren't here, I can call that devil whatever I want," Big Mother said.

"And he said to be respectful to us," Má retorted. "We are living here whether or not you like it."

Bé hid behind Má.

Big Mother harrumphed.

"Come," Má said, grabbing Bé's hand. "Bà Nội is waiting for us."

As they turned to go, Bé heard Big Mother yell at Xuân, "What did I tell you about getting dirty before dinner?"

"Don't look back," Má said. "He'll be okay."

Bé's stomach twisted as Big Mother continued to scream at Xuân. She wanted to cover her ears.

Bà Nội was waiting for them in their new bedroom. The room was spacious with a concrete floor and a large wooden bed by an open window.

Her grandmother was sitting on the bed, which was covered with an assortment of pretty dresses and house clothes in colorful patterns. There was also a pile of toys—an expensive-looking doll, paper lanterns, a silk hand fan, a set of marbles, and a bamboo flute.

"I have bought you some clothes and toys to make you comfortable," Bà Nội said.

"Thank you," Bé said shyly, still silently thinking of Xuân.

Later, at dinner, Bé sat between Bà Nội and Ba at the table. She squirmed uncomfortably as she looked back and forth between Má, who sat to Ba's right, and Big Mother, who was sitting across the table, surrounded by her sons. Neither woman said a word, but the silence could cut through steel. Má had a smile on her face as she ate, and Big Mother glared at her, eyes as cold as stone.

Bé looked over at Xuân, who was eating quietly, his head down, but Bé could see the purple bruise forming on his cheek.

Bà Nội kept adding pieces of grilled pork to Bé's rice bowl and urging her to eat.

"You're too skinny. Here, have some more meat," her grandmother said, adding the last piece of pork to her plate.

"That's not fair," her brother Bảo complained. "I worked in the paddy field today with Ba. I'm starving."

"Be nice to your sister. She's had a long journey," Bà Nội said, and Bảo gave Bé a murderous look. Bé looked down and ate quickly.

After everyone had finished their meal, Má brought out a huge plate of the ripe jackfruit for dessert. The boys reached for some, but Bà Nội slapped their hands. "Let your sister eat first."

The boys groaned, and Bà Nội pitted a large portion of the jackfruit and gave it to Bé. She hesitated, but her grandmother said, "Go on. Enjoy it. I hear it's your favorite fruit."

Bé looked at Má, who nodded, so Bé looked down and ate the sweet fruit, trying to ignore the angry eyes of her older brothers.

# CHAPTER 5

OVER THE NEXT several months, Bé adjusted to her life at Ba's house. Every morning, Má went to the paddy fields with Ba and Bé's oldest brothers to work, while Big Mother sold rice at the street market. Bà Nội stayed home to keep watch over the house and the property.

Xuân and Bé went to school during the day, but when they came home, they chased each other around their large property, played hide-and-seek in the chicken enclosure, climbed the tamarind tree at the front of the property, and took care of Bà Già the cat, who was getting plumper by the day from the food that Bé snuck her.

Sometimes the siblings went to play in the paddy

fields. Bà Nội always made them wear conical rice hats to protect their faces from the sun, though their arms and legs were dark from hours of playing outside.

Má kept Bé away from Big Mother, so Bé rarely saw her stepmother except for mealtimes. The two women didn't fight in front of Ba or Bà Nội, but whenever the wives were alone, they screamed and threw things at each other. Bé would watch with her head peeking out from the open doorway of the ancestral room.

Bé learned that Big Mother's temper was infamous in the village. No one dared to cross her, except for Ba, who fought with her when she was being too harsh to Má.

One afternoon, Bé walked barefoot along the raised narrow paths that separated the paddy fields, arms stretched out, balancing, careful not to fall in. Má watched nearby, muddy water up to her knees, reaching every few minutes for a rice seedling to transplant into the wet field. Ba worked in the field over, directing his workers and older sons.

Má looked close to tears. She never smiled anymore, so Bé waved at her like a wild child, smiling and leaping from one step to the next, mud splattering everywhere.

She twirled and jumped, hoping this would make her mother feel better.

"You are a terrible dancer, Little Sister," Xuân said.

"I'm better than you!" Bé harrumphed and stuck out her tongue.

He yawned. "I'm bored. Let's race!" Then he took off, yelling, "Pretend the Việt Cộng are coming. Run to that fork ahead! How fast can you run? Can you catch me?"

Bé ran after him, the cool mud squishing between her toes as the wind blew through her long hair. Then, she slipped on a muddy puddle and almost fell over into the paddy fields. She caught herself just in time, the bottom of her foot grazing over hard snail shells.

"Paddy snails!" Bé called out to Xuân, while leaning over and plucking one from the side of the raised path. Boiled snails were delicious dipped in ginger fish sauce.

For the rest of that afternoon, Bé and Xuân looked for snails in the mud. They leapt from one raised path to the next, climbed up and down dirt mounds—bare feet caked with mud and dirt. Bé felt only sunshine and happiness.

Eventually, they filled Xuân's rice hat three-fourths

full with freshwater paddy snails and a few crabs and small fish they'd caught. Bé looked at the muddy hat in Xuân's hands. She was scared Big Mother would be mad and punish Xuân for dirtying his rice hat. He saw her worry, but just shrugged, putting her at ease.

That afternoon was delicious. Bà Nội soaked the snails to get all the mud out, and Má cooked them with lemongrass, lime leaves, and ginger. Xuân and Bé ate like they were starving to death, juices running down their mouths. They competed to see who could eat the fastest. Their hands darted to each snail, digging the insides out with toothpicks, dipping them in sauce, chewing, and swallowing. The snails were chewy and a little rubbery, but the ginger gave them spice and flavor. It was the best-tasting food for the best day. "You are the best brother ever!" Bé said, and Xuân beamed.

After the perfect day of delicious paddy snails and running in the fields, Xuân and Bé were playing marbles in the front room of the house when Big Mother arrived home from selling in the market. Bé and Xuân exchanged looks and locked hands, ready to run.

Bé's heart thundered like a loud drum in her chest

as Big Mother stomped in from the adjoining outdoor kitchen, holding up Xuân's muddy rice hat. Her face was pinched in anger like a kettle about to blow.

"It's not his...," Bé explained, but Má quickly pulled her out of the room. She covered Bé's ears, but Bé could still hear Xuân's crying and Big Mother's yelling.

"It's all my fault," Bé sobbed as Má cradled her back and forth.

"Xuân is a big boy. He knew what he was doing with his hat," Má said, her eyes looking just as sad as Bé felt. "He knows what his mother is like."

Má brought dinner to their room that night. Ba came with her. Bé put her arms around him and squeezed. She couldn't help shaking.

Ba said, "Xuân is with your grandmother. She's rubbing tiger balm on him. He'll be all right by morning."

Bé frowned but nodded.

They sat on the floor and ate rice with caramelized fish, spinach soup, and stir-fried eggplant. The food warmed Bé's stomach and made her heart feel a little less heavy. Eating always helped Bé feel better. Má split open a mangosteen for Bé's dessert, and she gobbled it up in a few bites.

After dinner, Bé rinsed her body in front of the well, and Má washed Bé's long hair with willow bark water. Bé liked the feel of Ma's hands as she ran her fingers through her hair and massaged her scalp. After her hair was dry, Bé silently counted the brush strokes as Má brushed her hair. *Twenty-two, twenty-three, twenty-four.* She liked how the sheen of her black hair matched Má's, and how they both had strands of dark brown mixed in the black. They had identical hair, silky and smooth, that fell down their backs. Same eyes, same full lips. Bé liked being her mother's mini twin.

Má put the mosquito netting over the bed they shared, meticulously tucking the ends under the mattress, keeping the bugs out. She fanned Bé and told her bedtime stories about fairy queens and dragon kings. Bé fell asleep, cuddling up next to a soft blanket and listening to her mother's soft voice humming a sweet melody.

After that day, Xuân played with Bé less often, and when he did, he made sure that no one knew, not even his older brothers. Whenever they came home, he'd run to them instead of continuing to play with Bé.

# CHAPTER 6

THREE MONTHS LATER, on the second day of Tết—the lunar new year—Bà Nội took Bé and her brothers to visit Great-Uncle Five's house. He was Bà Nội's older brother and lived only three streets over.

Bà Nội walked slowly as they entered, leaning heavily on Trân for support. She'd become frailer in the last few months, and her skin was pale. Today, everyone wore their nicest clothes. Bé wore a red áo dài embroidered with flowers that matched her grandmother's outfit, and her brothers wore blue. Tết was one of the most important holidays of the year—a day you ate delicious food, visited relatives and close friends, and watched the unicorn and lion dance in the streets.

Bé had never been to Great-Uncle Five's house

before, and she was awed at all the animals he kept in cages on his terrace. There were birds and parrots of all colors and sizes, squawking loudly, fluttering around in their too-small birdcages hung up high. A macaque monkey leapt around in a large cage in a corner of the terrace, and a long snake was curled up within a glass enclosure.

The monkey looked adorable with its curious eyes, but when Bé stood too close to its cage, it grabbed and yanked her hair, hooting and laughing at her.

She screamed and pulled her hair back from the evil monkey. Her oldest brothers all laughed, and Bảo said, "That's what you get for having long hair."

Bé made a face at Bảo and looked over at Xuân, hoping he'd say something, but he ignored her, having become more distant with each passing month.

"Children!" Bà Nội snapped, her voice sounding worn out. "We are guests here. Let's not fight today. Bảo, apologize to your sister."

Bảo mumbled "Sorry" under his breath and then gave her an annoyed face when their grandmother looked away.

"Be careful with that monkey. He's spirited," Great-

Uncle Five said as he came out to greet the family. He was a short man with thick salt-and-pepper hair, and although he was three years older than Bà Nội, he had a youthful look about him. He was thin with taut arm muscles that showed under his short-sleeved shirt.

Bé and her siblings bowed and greeted their great-uncle, who motioned for Bà Nội to sit down on a bench on the terrace. He brought out a portable table and set out a white teapot and small cups.

"Sister, you don't look well. Is your son not taking good care of you?" Great-Uncle Five said, pouring the tea.

Bà Nội coughed dryly, and then took a sip of tea. "I am just tired. It's been a difficult transition with the two wives. I wish I had chosen better for him in the beginning. His first wife is . . ." She shook her head, then sighed.

"Everyone knows how his first wife is. She's got a big mouth . . . and an even fouler disposition," Great-Uncle Five said. Then he turned to look at Bé, who was standing behind her grandmother, surrounded by her brothers. "Is this your new granddaughter?"

"Oh yes," Bà Nội said, looking back. "Bé, come sit by me."

Bé did as her grandmother asked and sat tentatively at the edge of the bench. Bà Nội took her hand and gave it a squeeze. "She's a beautiful child, don't you agree?"

"Why, yes. Such a pretty child. Takes after her mother, doesn't she? I hear her mother is quite the beauty. Young, too, isn't she? Half your son's age?" Great-Uncle Five said.

Bà Nội nodded. "She is, but she's very helpful around the house. Takes very good care of me, especially now that I'm often fatigued and do not have the strength I used to."

"You must take care of your health, Sister," Great-Uncle Five said. Then he pulled a red lì xì packet from his pocket and said, "What do you say, child?"

Bé's face lit up. "I wish you good health and prosperity, and for you to live a very long time, Uncle."

He smiled at that and gave her the packet. "Now, boys, it's your turn."

One by one, Bé's brothers lined up and offered him

their good wishes for the upcoming year, and Great-Uncle Five gave them lucky money.

After this, the boys went off to play in Great-Uncle's yard, while Bà Nội continued visiting with her brother.

Bé called for Xuân to come over. As he did, he looked over his shoulder to make sure his other brothers weren't watching.

"I owe you half my lì xì money, remember? From racing to see who would gather the most eggs the day I came," Bé said.

"That was a long time ago, Little Sister. You can keep it and buy something nice for yourself," Xuân said.

"No, you should have it," Bé said, holding out the red envelope. "I promised, and I never break a promise."

Before Xuân could take it, Great-Uncle Five's pet monkey stuck his long hands through the cage bars and snatched it for himself, hooting and laughing at her as he cradled the envelope. Bé hadn't even realized she'd been standing close to the monkey cage.

"Hey!" she called out, jumping up to try to take her lucky money back. But the monkey's cage was too tall.

"Here, you can take mine," Xuân said. "I get lots of lì xì from my mother's side of the family."

He didn't say that Bé's mother had no family, so she'd automatically get less New Year's money. Bé appreciated that. He handed her the red envelope Great-Uncle Five had given him, and then ran off.

When it was time to leave, Bé gave the monkey a murderous glare, but he just laughed at her, still cradling her lucky money.

As the months passed, Bà Nội became weaker and less mobile. By the time the rainy season came that summer, she was confined to her bed with an ongoing cough that wouldn't go away. She was too weak to stand on her own, and Bé would sit with her in the afternoons after school. Bé would tell Bà Nội about her day, and about the rodents that her cat, Bà Già, had killed and brought her as a gift.

"It is good you have that cat to keep you company," Bà Nội said. "Continue to keep her a secret from your Big Mother. Protect her as much as you can."

Then Bà Nội said, "When I am gone, give comfort to your father, and continue to be dutiful to your mother.

Don't let Big Mother's mouth hurt you. Hide from her when you can."

"But you can't go, Bà Nội. You can still get better," Bé said.

Bà Nội touched her granddaughter's cheek. "Death comes to us all in the end. I am thankful for you, to have met you. I chose wrongly for your father. I should have picked another wife for him, but I am happy he chose your mother, so I can have you."

Bé leaned into Bà Nội's touch and smiled. "I love you, Bà Nội."

A few weeks later, Bà Nội died. Everyone had been sick with the flu and recovered. But her grandmother's frail body couldn't fight it off. She died in Ba's arms as he was carrying her to the doctor.

When Ba first broke the news, Má went white. The spoon she was holding fell into her hot soup with a *thunk*, the liquid spilling over its brim.

Bé, who was sick in bed, started to cry. "Bà Nội . . . g-gone."

Although her grandmother had tried to prepare her for her death, Bé felt the shock of it run through her body, and she couldn't stop the tears.

Má's eyes filled with worry. She rubbed Bé's back and said, "Shhhhh, it's going to be okay. Breathe."

Bé watched the spilled soup pool and soak into their mattress. Má didn't notice.

Má whispered to Ba, "Big Sister will be head of the household now . . . What does that mean for me? What about Thương?"

Ba wrapped his arms around Má and Bé and said, "Nothing will change."

# CHAPTER 7

THE NEXT MORNING, Bé watched in the corner as Big Mother and Má stripped Bà Nội of the clothes she had died in and changed her into the burial outfit she had chosen beforehand. Bà Nội's body looked bloated and lifeless, and her skin had lost its color. *Do all dead bodies look like this?* Bé wondered.

Xuân sat next to Bé and held her hand. They were silent, but her mind was full of questions. *Who will comfort Xuân now?* Bà Nội had been the one to love Xuân when his mother didn't, and now she was gone forever.

They laid Bà Nội on a bed covered with rose petals. Everyone was crying, tears soaking their traditional white mourning outfits. The white cloth Má had tied to Bé's forehead was tight, but no one else complained about their funeral head wraps, so Bé kept quiet.

Later, at the cemetery, Má cried loudly as they lowered Bà Nội's coffin into the ground. Xuân and Bé looked down at the hole where Bà Nội would rest forever. It was deep in the ground and the soil was dark and shadowy. It scared Bé. She was afraid she'd fall in, imagining herself in the hole, the dirt suffocating her lungs. She watched her uncles throw dirt over the grave, and she stumbled backward.

It wasn't long after the funeral when the screaming fights between Má and Big Mother became worse. They even fought in front of Ba, who was so worn down from grief over his mother's death that he didn't even try to stop them.

Ba had said nothing would change, but it felt like everything was changing—like nothing would ever be the same, like things would only get worse. Ba still went to work in the fields with Má every morning, but when he returned home, he went straight to his room to rest. It was as if Bà Nội's death had sapped him of his energy.

Má looked tired all the time, and she had developed dark circles under her eyes.

Big Mother, on the other hand, had never looked happier, as she was the matriarch of the house now. Her cheeks were full of color, and her face always seemed to be in a blissful state, even when she yelled at Má. She found the smallest things to fight about, from Má making too much rice for dinner to the fish being under-seasoned. Sometimes, she'd even smack Má across the face. Má cried herself to sleep every night, and Bé didn't know what to do. She snuggled with her until Bé fell asleep.

To make matters worse, Xuân disappeared com-pletely, only emerging during mealtimes. He snuck away to hidden corners on the property, or he spent time with neighborhood friends, but he was rarely home.

Bé had been right, and things only became worse.

Three weeks after the funeral, a stroke struck Ba down in the paddy fields as he worked. He fell off the water buffalo he was riding and straight into the muddy waters. At first, he couldn't move the left side of his body, and he was in bed for a month. Bé was worried.

All she could think of was whether he was going to live or die.

Má and Bé sat at his bedside day and night. Má cooked him healing rice porridge and spoon-fed him because he was too weak to feed himself. Bé fanned him until her arms got too tired. At night, they slept cuddled up next to him, clinging onto hope.

Bé's brothers worked harder than ever in the fields, working late into the evening, and they came to visit Ba once a day to tell him of their progress.

Never once did Big Mother come to visit him. Once a week, she would ask if he was dead yet. Bé didn't understand how she could be so cruel.

To Bé's great relief, Ba survived his stroke, but he was not the same.

Once, Ba had been brawny and strong as a water buffalo. His face had been round and glowed with health, muscles had framed his broad shoulders, and his dark tan skin had glistened in the sun. He'd radiated strength and vigor. He could plow a field without any help. He could axe down an entire bamboo grove with little trouble. He had hand-built the trellises for the loofa squash that grew in the garden. But that Ba was gone. His stroke had left him feeble and weak. He was no longer able to stand up to Big Mother, who now ruled the house without anyone tempering her anger.

To Bé's surprise, Má stopped fighting with Big Mother. Instead, she grew quiet. She spent most of her time sleeping when she didn't have to work. She brought meals to the room she shared with Bé but didn't eat much. Bé noticed that her clothes were becoming baggy, and her frame was getting smaller and smaller. Bé wished she knew how to comfort her mother, and she longed for someone to ask, but Bà Nội was gone, and Ba was still recovering from his stroke. *I'll find a way to make things better. I'll help Má and Ba*, Bé thought, determined.

One evening, Má took Bé's hand and walked her to the terrace where the full moon was just peeking out of the clouds. Má wrapped Bé in her arms, cradling her like she did when Bé was a baby. "Do you remember the story of Chú Cuội, the man on the moon?"

Bé shook her head.

"A long, long time ago, Chú Cuội lived on earth.

There was a special banyan tree in his yard, and Chú Cuội told his wife never to plant flowers near the root of that tree," Má began.

Bé closed her eyes, imagining a banyan tree, huge and green.

"But she loved flowers too much, so one day when he was off in the jungle, she planted some dahlias by the tree and her trowel accidentally cut off one of its roots."

"No!" Bé exclaimed.

"The tree was magic, you see, and it started growing bigger and bigger and pulling its roots from the ground. Chú Cuội's wife started screaming, and Chú Cuội came running just as his special tree was pulling its last root from the ground and rising up to the sky. He tried to pull the tree back to the earth, but the banyan was too strong for him, and it pulled Chú Cuội all the way up to the moon."

"How did he get back?" Bé asked. "What happened to his wife?"

"He didn't," Má said. "The banyan tree flew up to the moon and sank its roots in the sparkling moon dust. And now, years and years later, Chú Cuội is still there, looking down at the earth, missing his wife, and wanting a way home."

Bé's stomach clenched. "So he's just stuck there? On the moon?"

Má nodded. "Whenever you look up at the full moon, sometimes you can see a tiny figure of a man leaning against a tree, playing his flute." Má pointed to the large moon above, shining brightly in the dark night.

Then, against Bé's ear, Má whispered ever so softly, "When I go, I will miss you and I'll always look for a way back to you. I promise."

*Go?* Bé didn't understand what Má meant, but she hoped no one would ever end up like Chú Cuội.

# CHAPTER 8

Bé CLUNG onto Má for dear life. She laced her fingers together and wound them tight around Má's waist, crying inconsolably. Bé couldn't believe that the story her mother had told her the night before was coming true.

Má stood on the terrace with a packed bag while Big Mother stood nearby, smiling.

"You are fierce like a tiger," Má said. "You are the most courageous daughter. I know you will grow up stronger than I ever was. And you will survive, even without me for a time."

"No, Má . . . Please take me with you!"

Má's eyes, a rich brown like Bé's, creased at the

corners. She said, "Sometimes in life, we have to make impossible choices. I cannot stay here, and there's no life yet for you where I am going."

"But, Má . . ." Bé sobbed.

"One day, when the war is over, we will live in a new place together. A house at the top of the mountains, where you can see the forest and sea below us. A house so large we can get lost in it. Where you can eat all the pastries and food you want and have all the toys your heart desires. A place where all your dreams can come true. How would you like that?"

Bé sniffed. "Yes, I would love that."

"Until then, be brave. Have strength." She then leaned down and whispered, "Don't show Big Mother your weakness. She will only use it against you." Then she kissed her daughter's forehead, her lips soft and warm against Bé's skin. "Promise you won't come looking for me. The world is a very dangerous place."

Má brushed a tendril of tear-soaked hair from Bé's face and gave her one last embrace. "When I save enough, make enough money, I will come back here. I will come back for you. I promise."

Bé wished Ba was home. He would have stopped her. But he was in the village, visiting the doctor, and Má was leaving.

"Be strong and brave for me," Má said. "Take care of her, Big Sister."

Big Mother took hold of Bé's shoulder and held her in place. "My husband's daughter will be cherished. Everything will be as we agreed."

*What agreement?* Bé's eyebrows furrowed, confused.

"She's lying, Má! Don't believe her!" Bé yelled, but Má was already turning away.

"No!" Bé screamed, struggling against Big Mother's grip as she watched Má leave. Big Mother's meaty hands dug into her arms, but she squirmed this way and that, her feet sliding in the dirt.

"Má!"

Finally, Bé's feet found purchase, and she stomped down on her stepmother's foot. Hard. The woman yelped and released her.

Bé took off in the direction Má had gone, heart aching, nerves a jumbled mess. Soon she was outside their property in the busy street, lost in the flurry of traffic. Bicycles, xích lô pedicabs, and mopeds whirled around her, narrowly avoiding her. People yelled for her to get out of the road. Bé turned in a circle, not sure which way Má had gone, looking in every direction. The street was chaos. Then she spotted Má stepping onto a xe đò bus, crammed tight with too many bodies, over-loaded with luggage and baskets full of people's posses-sions piled on top. She yelled for Má, but she was too far away. The road was too noisy with the morning rush for Má to hear her. Má didn't turn around, only squeezed her way into the bus, and then it chugged down the street.

Bé ran after the bus, dodging bicycles, people pull-ing carts of merchandise, and women walking. There were too many vehicles on the road, and the bus was moving too fast for Bé's legs to keep up. Soon the xe đò bus was gone, joined by other xe đò in the distance.

Má was gone.

*Crack . . . crack.* Something was fracturing inside her.

Bé stood there in the street, staring at all the bicycles and vehicles, all the ways people could travel, lost in the chaos.

It wasn't long before Big Mother was upon her, the veins on her neck protruding, screaming something about obedience and respecting your elders. But Bé couldn't hear her. She was kilometers away, on that bus with Má.

Big Mother dragged Bé to the house, holding a fistful of her hair. She felt the pulling, but the pain was muted—like she had left her body and was watching from far away as her stepmother pulled some other girl's hair, hurling curses and profanities. Soon Xuân was behind his mother, pleading for her to stop, trying to grab Bé.

Big Mother let go once they reached the terrace. Bé lost her balance and her knee knocked hard against the brick well near the front of the house. Xuân tried to help Bé up, tried to comfort her, but she couldn't hear him. She was lost somewhere above, watching.

"You! Get out!" Big Mother pointed something sharp at Xuân. He stumbled backward.

Bé's eyes focused on the glinting, sharp object. A knife. Big Mother had a knife in her hand. Bé wanted to run but was too afraid.

"Who did she think she was? Stealing my husband, giving birth to a devil, coming into my house. Good riddance!" Big Mother screamed. "And just look at you. You're the spitting image of her. But don't worry, I'm going to change that!"

Big Mother stood over Bé with the knife. Bé flinched. Xuân screamed. The woman grabbed a piece of Bé's hair and sliced through her tresses. Bé's mouth fell open as piece by piece, the strands of her once long hair fell to the ground like a waterfall.

When Big Mother was done, she smiled. "Ah, that's better. Not even your mother would recognize you now."

Bé ran as fast as she could to the room she had shared with her mother and grabbed a mirror.

"My hair . . ." Her voice faded, choked. She touched what was left. A jagged, uneven mess that was short around her ears and a little longer in the back met her fingertips. She was not her mother's mini twin anymore. She looked like a boy. Her long, silky, ebony hair, hair that was identical to her mother's, hair that Má washed every day and brushed every night, was gone.

Gone like Má.

Gone like Bà Nội.

The mirror in Bé's hand slipped and clattered to the ground. Xuân found his sister minutes later. He let her cry and cry on his shoulder until she had no tears left to shed and no voice to speak. There was nothing left to say. Her true name had been taken from her. Her mother was gone. Who was she now? She was nothing.

"Bé, what can I do? How can I help?" Xuân asked.

When she opened her mouth, nothing came out. Not even a squeak. She was completely mute.

"Bé, say something. Anything." Xuân tried to coax her voice out of her, but it was gone. Disappeared along with her hair, along with Má's bus, lost in the ether.

*Crack . . . crack . . .*

Something inside Bé shattered, like porcelain when the temperature changes too quickly, when dropped by clumsy hands, when thrown by monkeys, exploding into a million tiny shards with no hope of being glued back together.

PART 2

# SOUR TAMARIND, CRACKED PORCELAIN

# CHAPTER 9

Bé HID HIGH in the tamarind tree, lush and heavy with young fruit too sour to eat, her legs dangling from the branch. No one could see her, but she could see them: the wary and tired South Vietnamese soldiers on patrol in their dusty uniforms with long rifles, villagers riding by on bicycles and motorbikes.

The tree's thick limbs and green oval-shaped leaves, bushy and protective, kept the house from sight and away from the war that crept closer and closer with each passing day. The feeling in the village had become especially tense since the assassination of the South Vietnamese president, Ngô Đình Diệm, last November.

There had been recent news that the Việt Cộng were

pillaging homes in nearby hamlets in their district, their flamethrowers burning down thatched houses of poor villagers, and grenades thrown into safety bunkers. Many people died. So far, the South Vietnamese Army and their village outpost had been successful at keeping the communists away from Bé's village. But as the civil war waged on, everyone lived in fear that their village would be next. Ba always said you never knew when the Việt Cộng could arrive.

Yet, life was still prosperous in Bé's village. People had enough to eat. They bought and sold in the market like normal, and life went on as it always had. Bé watched the village women as they carried huge baskets of produce to the chợ chồm hỗm street market. She searched the face of each woman who passed, desperately hoping one of them was Má. But it never was.

It had been seven months and five days since she saw her mother. She wound the memories of Má tight inside like a taut spool of thread. Maybe if she held the memories close enough, Má would never slip away.

It was Má's voice that Bé missed the most, honeyed and soft like the wind as it blew against water lilies on calm summer days. Its sound became more muted with each day she was gone, quieter and softer. *Will it soon fade away altogether? What if there is only a dull noise left where Má's soft voice used to be?* The thought scared Bé.

Bé's stomach ached with hunger. She had eaten nothing since the day before yesterday, when Ba was away. Big Mother had flung hot oil at her, burning her leg. Bé had been hiding ever since.

During the day, she'd hidden in the chicken coop enclosure, behind the tall hay mound. It was there that she took care of Bà Già and her new family. Bà Già had given birth to the cutest litter of kittens, and they'd become Bé's treasured babies.

For two nights, Bé slept at the back of the pigsty, snuggling with the pigs she'd raised since they were piglets. Bé knew it wasn't safe to be outside at night because of the Việt Cộng. But Big Mother wasn't safe either. So if the Việt Cộng did come, the last place they might look was a pigsty. At least, that's what she hoped. In the mornings, she climbed high in the tree, letting the bushy leaves shield her.

Bé picked a green, raw tamarind fruit from the limb

above her head and nibbled on it. She winced at the sour taste, but it calmed her angry belly. Bé's ragged clothes were damp from the blistering humid heat, and she reeked. She didn't mind though. She was safe.

It was lucky that the rainy season would not come for a few more months. For now, the weather was hot and dry, but when the rains came, Bé wouldn't be able to hide outside.

She closed her eyes and savored the peaceful moment. The leaves rustled slightly in the breeze, fanning her like Má used to do at night, rolling in memories to comfort her.

Bé liked escaping into her memories. Some of her best were of Xuân, but her half-brother never played with her anymore. Big Mother's punishments had become especially cruel for Xuân after he had tried to protect Bé from a beating. Since then, Xuân didn't even try to speak to Bé—not that she would respond back with words. She had no desire to speak. And even if she did, there was no voice to speak them. Bé's voice had disappeared when her mother left, seven months and five days ago. Since then, she'd spoken to no one.

Not to Xuân. Not to Ba. Not even to herself when she was alone.

Still, Bé was glad Xuân had made her chase him all those times, even if she hadn't been able to outrun Big Mother the day before yesterday. Bé looked down at her burned leg where the blisters from the hot oil had begun to form. Big Mother's punishments always left a mark.

She looked at her brown, tattered shirt and matching-colored cotton pants that ended just below her knees. Her clothes were becoming tight, and she knew she'd only be able to wear them for a little while longer.

*Will Big Mother buy me new clothes?* she wondered. *Probably not.* She was sure to wear her big brothers' hand-me-downs.

Bé missed the days when she had worn the brand-new outfits that Bà Nội had bought for her, but those days were long gone. Her clothes and everything else— her khai sinh, a birth certificate with her real name, along with all of Má's paperwork and the possessions she'd left behind—had been burned in a huge bonfire at the back of the property. Big Mother had even burned the mattress she and Má had slept on, their family photographs, and every gift that Bé had ever received from Ba and Bà Nội. Everything was gone in an instant. Big Mother had kept only the ugliest outfits, and at eleven years old, Bé was quickly outgrowing them.

The aroma of freshly baked bread from a passing bánh mì sandwich cart pulled Bé from her thoughts. It was almost lunchtime. Back at the house, Big Mother would be cooking for her sons, and Ba would come looking for her soon. He never allowed her to stay away for too long.

Bé relaxed against the tree's trunk. She was going nowhere. Bé watched the light as it dappled through the leaves of her tree. The bright sun hung high above the cloudless day. Her feet swung, the leaves above her rustled lightly with a passing breeze, and she watched the tree's tamarind fruits sway like they were dancing without a care. She'd rather keep remembering, even if the memories were both salty and sweet, good mixed with bad.

Before long, Ba was in the distance, walking slowly toward her, hesitantly, leaning heavily on his cane, just like how Bà Nội used to. Ba had aged ten years in less than one. His muscles were gone. His skin was taut against the bones in his neck and chest. His face was sunk into itself, deep wrinkles curled tight. He stood permanently hunched, his spine curved, each bone protruding outward—a walking skeleton. His white shirt dangled loosely over his too-skinny frame like he was a child playing dress-up. His dark pants were pulled all the way up over his stomach, the belt looped on the tightest hole.

Ba had to stop a few times to catch his breath on his way to the tamarind tree. It was a sad sight for Bé. She often thought that if the wind blew too strongly, Ba would topple over. It was lucky that he mostly stayed inside during monsoon season.

"Con," Ba said, looking up into the branches. These days, he always called her "con," a word that meant "child." Big Mother only called her "it" or "devil." Never again would she be called by her true name. Knowing this left a bitter taste in her mouth.

Even with Ba down below, shaded by the tree's branches, Bé didn't budge from her perch. She didn't want to leave the safety of her tree.

"Con, you need to eat. You've skipped three meals. I don't want you to starve," Ba said. "How about a bánh bao?"

Ba waved a bánh bao in the air. Bé's stomach growled loudly just at that moment, and her mouth watered at the memory of steaming bánh bao—the steamed pork buns that were once her favorite breakfast food, back before everything changed.

Bé couldn't escape her fate. She knew that she'd have to face her stepmother sooner or later. Reluctantly, she climbed down from the tree and stood silently before her father. He handed her the bánh bao, and together, arm in arm, they walked very slowly back up to the house in silence, taking their time.

It was a five-minute walk from the tamarind tree to the house.

With each step, Bé relished the slightly sweet taste of the bánh bao dough and the savory bites of ground pork and egg. Her stomach welcomed the food happily. When the small pork bun was gone, she was still hungry, but the bun had helped. Ba patted her arm, and she smiled. His face was withered like an aged bitter melon, with deep lines and creases, but his eyes were always warm. Like Bà Nội's eyes had been.

"Have strength," Ba said when they neared the house.

Bé looked up and braced herself.

## CHAPTER 10

Big Mother stood on the outdoor terrace in front of their house, wearing an ugly áo bà ba outfit—a brown, button-down silk shirt with long sleeves and black silk pants. The shirt was tight around her large midsection and made her look like a squeezed balloon. She stood with her hands clenched at her sides, scowling. "THERE YOU ARE!"

Bé pressed her lips together and stared defiantly at her stepmother.

"YOU LAZY LITTLE DEVIL!" Big Mother tore Bé away from Ba, making him stumble and nearly fall into the dirt. She pulled Bé hard toward the house. Bé tried to scramble away, cringing at her stepmother's sharp grip, but Big Mother wouldn't loosen her grasp.

"Wife, please," Ba said. "She needs to eat."

"She can starve for all I care!" Big Mother screeched. "I sit in that market day after day, my life always in danger, while this one daydreams!" She dug her sharp nails into Bé's arm. Bé struggled against her.

Bé saw the lines on Ba's forehead wrinkle, and a wave of sadness seemed to pour over his hunched body.

Big Mother turned and spat at the ground. Bé stared at Big Mother's round face marred with heavy wrinkles, sunken eyes, and dark sunspots. Big Mother wasn't beautiful. *Not like Má*, Bé thought, and she took comfort in this.

Big Mother forced Bé down to the ground in front of the outdoor kitchen and dining area where the rest of the family was eating at a wooden table. Ba tried to intervene, but he was unsteady on his feet. Big Mother screamed, "Leave her! Go sit with your real family."

Ba tried to argue again, but Big Mother dragged him over to her brothers at the table.

Bé didn't follow Ba and Big Mother. She knew where she was forced to eat. She sat outside in the heat, next to the dogs that Big Mother had adopted six months ago to guard the property.

"Eat!" Big Mother said, tossing a ceramic bowl of rice toward her. Bé quickly caught the bowl. She knew that if the bowl broke, she'd have to eat the rice from the cracked tile ground. Big Mother didn't give her any chopsticks, and there was nothing in her bowl but a tiny portion of white rice mixed with fish sauce and sliced red chili peppers. Spicy food hurt Bé's stomach and Big Mother knew this.

Bé picked out the chili peppers from the rice, flicked them to the ground, and began to eat. The rice was still spicy from where the chilies had touched it and the spice made her nose run, but she forced herself to chew and swallow. As she did her best to eat, Bé listened to her brothers gossip about the war. They were boisterous, each voice talking over the other.

"The rumor is the Americans were involved in the coup that killed President Diệm," Bảo yelled as he ate. "And now they're here."

"No one wants the American imperialists here. This isn't their country. This isn't their war. The Việt Cộng are calling us puppet troops, a puppet government," Trân chimed in, his voice seething with anger. "Nhật told me our troops are losing morale."

Ba sighed. "We are lost. This land is still ours, but as the Việt Cộng win battles and conquer more areas, they are taking land away from the rightful owners. If the Việt Cộng were able to root out the South Vietnamese Army stationed in our village . . . whether now or in the future, the Việt Cộng will win our country. The Americans have destroyed our just cause."

Bé shuddered, not wanting to think about what a world ruled by the Việt Cộng would look like.

Everyone had heard the rumors of what happened to villages taken over by the Việt Cộng. Many were killed, even random villagers, just to prove that no one was safe unless they gave their full cooperation. Everyone was forced to work for the Việt Cộng. Older men and women were made to move supplies and sabotage roads by planting landmines and bombs. Younger men were made to fight in their army, or they would volunteer out of fear for their families' safety.

The Việt Cộng also made villagers pay heavy taxes, in the form of rice, and tattle on their neighbors. If you didn't go along with what the Việt Cộng wanted, or if they thought you were working secretly for the South Vietnamese Army, you could end up dead or taken away from your home. With this threat, most grew less rice in the paddy fields, only producing enough to feed their families. Some ran away to live in southern hamlets, villages, and cities that were protected by the South Vietnamese Army.

Bé usually liked listening to all Nhật's and Văn's terrible stories when they visited home on their two-week holiday from soldiering, but today Bé couldn't help but tune her brothers out. Her focus was solely on the aroma of grilled meat and caramelized black-pepper fish that moved quickly from their bowls into their mouths. Her stomach grumbled as she watched her brothers gorge themselves on meat and fish.

Bé eyed the dogs' food bowl. Even they were given pieces of meat and fat mixed in with leftover rice from yesterday's meal. When the dogs wandered away, Bé reached over and grabbed a handful of rice and meat from their bowl and shoved it into her mouth. She tasted roasted meat mixed with slimy dog saliva and dirt, but that was better than still being hungry and the meat tasted good. She put some in her pocket to save for her cat family and then reached for more.

Bé's hand was still in the bowl when Trân tattled. "She's a dog, Mother." He laughed, and then the entire table erupted into laughter. *Is Xuân laughing too?*

Embarrassed, Bé dropped the handful and stared into her own bowl.

"Leave her be," Ba said. "Be kind to the child."

"Why?" Trân said. "Her mother didn't want her and neither do we."

"Yeah, let the Việt Cộng have her!" chimed in Bảo.

Xuân was silent, and Bé wished he would defend her. He would have in the old days. He glanced at Bé, his eyes somber.

She missed Xuân so much it hurt.

Tears threatened to form in Bé's eyes, not from the spicy rice, but because she remembered all too well how things used to be before Má left, when Xuân was still her best friend, and she was surrounded by love.

Bé swallowed the lump in her throat. She refused to let herself cry. Instead, she stared down at her tattered shirt, focusing on an old brownish mud stain. She thought about scrubbing and scrubbing until it disappeared.

She reminded herself of Má's promise to her the day she left. Bé didn't want the toys anymore, but she held onto the dream of a loving home and a mother to comfort her.

"Con," Ba whispered. Bé glanced up to see him standing over her. Big Mother wasn't anywhere in sight. Ba handed her a rice bowl with grilled meat shredded into small pieces in exchange for her empty bowl.

Later, when her stepmother returned, Bé had finished the bowl of rice Ba had given her and the woman knew nothing.

# CHAPTER 11

AFTER LUNCH, Big Mother loaded the rear of her bicycle with three large bags of rice from the fields and headed to the street market to sell, while Ba and Bé's brothers enjoyed an afternoon nap. Bé was never allowed to take a nap. There was always too much for her to do.

Big Mother didn't allow Bé to go to school anymore, so Bé was responsible for doing all the household chores.

Bé squatted on the ground near the old brick well, scrubbing dirty dishes with soap and water in a metallic bowl. After the dishes were done, she washed the family's laundry using water from the well in a plastic tub of soapy water. She hung the clothes to dry on a clothesline next to the house.

Then it was time for her other chores.

Every day, Bé watered the vegetable and herb garden, and she harvested the ripe vegetables and herbs for their meals. The extras were sold at the market or were mixed into the pigs' slop. Next to the garden were two empty plots of land saved for her elder brothers to build homes on when they eventually married. Daughters were never saved plots of land, as they always went to live with their husbands.

Across the dirt courtyard where the small coconut trees grew, Bé's family raised five grown pigs and their piglets in an enclosed brick pigsty. When the pigs were fat enough, Big Mother sold them to be slaughtered. Every day, Bé carried the heavy bucket of pig slop to the pigsty, where she watered and fed them.

After taking care of the pigs, Bé would grab a basket of chicken feed from the house and a cup of water and would rush to the chicken enclosure at the back of their property. There she would feed the chickens and check on her cat family. She was careful not to spill the water as she worked.

Bé scurried through the courtyard, past the pigsty,

through another barren plot of land being saved for Xuân, and toward the chicken enclosure in the back, where she and Xuân used to play when they were younger. The memory of their happy times haunted the place like a ghost, and Bé ached for him.

Bà Già had dug a hole inside the mound for her kittens, so Bé pushed the hay aside to see the family better. The mother cat was lying on her side as her five kittens suckled. There was a hiss, but when Bà Già saw it was Bé, the black cat purred. Bé grabbed the saved rice from her pocket and placed it next to Bà Già's head, and she refilled Bà Già's water bowl with the water she brought.

Bé watched the runt of the litter—a tiny little thing with distinctive striped gray fur—clawing, trying to squeeze in between his siblings for some milk. Bà Già bent her face toward him and gave him a lick. He was Bé's favorite. He was like her, ignored by his other siblings but still loved by Bà Già. Bé decided to name the runt Mèo.

Her cat family warmed her heart. Bé petted all the new kittens, enjoying the feeling of their soft new fur against her calloused fingers. These kittens were so new in the world, so loved, and so whole.

*Seven months and five days ago, I was whole, too,* Bé thought. She had laughed, told stories, dreamed, and played without a care in the world.

As a passing breeze blew a piece of Bé's short hair toward her face, she wished she could tell Xuân about the kittens. They would care for them together like they did for Bà Già, but he never came to the chicken enclosure anymore. She'd lost him along with everything else.

She stayed in the chicken yard as long as she could watching her cats, but it was getting late, and Bé still had more to do. She picked up tiny Mèo and cuddled him before leaving. The newly born kitten made the cutest squealing sound. It made Bé grin. After giving him a final kiss, she put him down next to his siblings and covered the cat den with loose hay.

Bé then scattered the feed and checked the chicken enclosure to make sure that the stray dog she had scared away last week wasn't around. Her cats gave her something to look forward to every day, and Bé would protect them at all costs.

Walking back to the house, a loud commotion drew her attention to the street. One of the neighbors, Chi Yen, ran into the courtyard screaming, "They took the baby! The monkeys have taken my baby! Help!" She was frantic with wild eyes, hair flying everywhere. Her wails were so loud that Bé's brothers woke up and emerged from the house, rubbing sleep from their eyes.

"Con khỉ! The macaque monkeys!" Chi Yen made a furious gesture for them to follow. "My baby! The monkeys stole my baby!"

Bé dropped the basket she was carrying and ran after her. Her brothers outran her and were in the street before she even made it to her tamarind tree. Ahead of her, Xuân slowed his pace and waited for her to catch up. He grabbed her hand, and they ran out together.

It felt good to hold his hand.

They followed the crowd onto the main street, where Chi Yen's family was shouting, rallying people to help. There was a mob of people already assembled, and Xuân and Bé were quickly swallowed by bodies. Many of the shops, as well as food and merchandise stands that lined the road, were closed—their owners at home taking their customary afternoon naps. A few bicycles and motorbikes weaved around the crowd. Some stopped to see what the commotion was all about.

"His sister was watching him when the monkeys came. They taunted the girl, pulled at her clothes, and she ran off, scared. Then the macaques took the baby!" Chi Yen's grandmother said to the crowd.

"Macaques are nothing but trouble," said a tall man who stood next to Bé.

"To Dồi Khỉ! To Monkey Hill!" chanted the crowd.

Then people were running, or riding on bicycles and mopeds, kicking up a cloud of dust and dirt as they went. Bé saw the uniforms of at least seven South Vietnamese soldiers running with the crowd.

Bé ran with Xuân, her pulse racing a million kilometers a minute, pumping her arms and running as fast as she could, stretching her calves to their limit. It felt good to run with her brother, just like old times, even if she had grown slightly taller. She felt free. She felt strong.

They ran toward the village center, through the chợ chồm hỗm street market, angry voices on all sides:

some chanted the call to help find the baby, others screamed about their trampled produce and ruined food. Xuân and Bé kept their heads down and pumped their legs even faster. They didn't want to run into Big Mother. The crowd rounded a corner, and brother and sister were running free by rice paddy fields. Bé's gaze lingered on the green fields and the mountains behind it. She squeezed Xuân's hand and thought of her old life and that day they'd caught and eaten snails.

Behind the paddy field workers, clusters of uni-formed soldiers patrolled the fields. The mountains where the Việt Cộng were rumored to hide loomed in the distance. Bé shuddered, thinking about how close the Việt Cộng were and how dangerous it would be to run away from home. If she ran, where would she go? Would the Việt Cộng catch her and harm her? She didn't know where her mother was, and if she went back to her old village, where she and Má once lived, who would take her in? *Sang has probably forgotten about me by now, and the neighbors wouldn't want an extra burden when they're already struggling*, Bé thought. *Still, I wish I could run away.*

"I see the monkeys! And the baby!" yelled a man at the front of the crowd.

The crowd started their ascent up a hill and into the jungle. Everyone came to an abrupt stop at Dồi Khỉ— Monkey Hill, which sat at the mouth of the jungle.

The jungle was dark. Tall trees, vines, and lush vegetation surrounded them. Tree roots were exposed on the forest floor, surrounded by dead leaves and moss, and the ground was rocky in places. Sunlight filtered through the canopy, giving just enough light to see that, above the crowd, there were monkeys in every tree. Bé saw families of monkeys watching her overhead. They squeaked and chattered, and several emitted loud, high-pitched noises that sounded like screaming.

No one ventured any deeper into the forest than Monkey Hill. The villagers had been warned about the Việt Cộng strongholds in the forest, landmines hidden in unexpected places. There was an evil feeling to the place that made Bé shiver.

"My baby!" cried Chi Yen's voice.

*BOOOOOOOOM!*

The deafening sound of a cannon made the crowd

jump. Xuân pulled Bé to him, and she clung to his arm. The monkeys clambered up higher in the trees, squeaking loudly as they went.

"Who shot that?" someone asked.

"The Việt Cộng are here!" yelled a woman, her voice wavering in fear.

Everyone trembled as the rumor spread like wildfire, each eyeing the person standing next to them suspiciously.

"Quiet down!" announced a South Vietnamese soldier with a commanding voice. "The Việt Cộng are not here! It's only the artillery unit stationed here firing their cannons."

"My baby!" Chi Yen's voice called. Bé could hear her voice but not see her. "Thank Buddha! He's safe!" A baby cried, and everyone cheered.

Relief washed over Bé, but then she thought about Má and frowned.

Xuân stood on his tiptoes to see over the heads of everyone else. "The monkeys left the baby on the ground. He doesn't look like he's in too bad shape. The family is crowding all around him. It's over."

People turned to leave. Bé tripped over an empty cooking pan next to a fallen vine. The monkeys above taunted her, chattering in their monkey language, laughing and hollering.

She scowled. She thought about the evil monkey that Great-Uncle Five had as a pet—the one that pulled her hair and stole her lì xì, lucky New Year's money, from her hand. She hated monkeys.

Bé realized that along with the rocks and leaves, the ground of Monkey Hill was littered with all kinds of strange items—chopsticks, clothing, pots and pans, kerosene lamps, a little Buddha statue. A string of beautiful jade beads caught her attention. Bé picked it up. Each rounded bead was a pretty shade of green, connected at the end with a cross of a skinny man's outstretched arms. Bé ran her fingers over the smooth beads. *Are these real jade?* The strand reminded her of the jade bracelet that Ba had given Má. *I wonder if she still wears it.*

"Do you know what that is?" asked a man standing next to her.

She looked up and shook her head. It was the local priest. She had seen him on Sunday mornings, walking in and out of the poorest houses in the neighborhood. He was young with slick black hair, and he always wore the same outfit—all black with a little bit of white on his collar. Bé wondered if he ever got hot in his black clothes.

"It's a rosary," the priest said. "It's mine, actually. The naughty monkeys stole it last week. I knew I'd find it here."

Bé offered it back to him, but he shook his head. "Would you like it?"

She blinked, wishing words would come from her mouth but not knowing what to say if they did. The string of beads was pretty, but she wouldn't know what to do with it.

"My sister doesn't speak," Xuân explained.

The priest nodded his understanding. "Keep it. It is my gift to you."

"Thank you, Cha," Xuân said, and Bé bowed.

"It's a necklace of hope and prayer for the impossible to come true," Cha said. "Keep it safe. We need hope, especially in times like these. Your mother would want you to have it."

*He knew my mother?* As if reading her thoughts, Xuân asked the priest the same question.

"Yes," Cha said, gesturing for the two to walk with him. "I was the parish priest in your hometown, Thương, for many years, before the diocese moved me to take over the church here. Your mother was an orphan. Her parents died when she was a child, and I tried to help her as best as I could."

Bé's eyes lit up at hearing her real name.

"She came to me before . . ." Cha's voice trailed off. Then he took Bé's hand and patted it. "It would break your mother's heart to know how badly you're being treated."

"Does everyone know?" Xuân asked.

"Your mother loves to gossip," Cha said. "Everyone knows how much she hates Thương."

Then Cha turned to Bé and said, "Your mother loved you, Thương. She thought that by leaving, you would have a chance of a better life. Your stepmother made many promises to your mother that she never intended to keep."

Bé nodded, already knowing this. She wondered if

Cha knew where her mother had gone. *Do you know where Má is?* Bé asked silently, wishing the words would come out of her mouth. She knew they wouldn't.

They reached the tamarind tree, and Cha said, "Keep the rosary safe."

Bé nodded, and she promised to herself she would.

"Hide it. Don't let my mother see. She hates Catholics," Xuân said. Then he ran ahead, leaving Bé alone by her tamarind tree.

# CHAPTER 12

That evening, Big Mother came home grumpier than usual, complaining about the dust that the passing crowd kicked up during their haste to rescue the baby. Someone had knocked over three baskets of rice and made a mess in Big Mother's stall. The white rice had fallen to the ground, and she had spent the rest of the afternoon rinsing the dirt from the kernels.

None of Bé's brothers admitted to running with the crowd.

Big Mother pointed a finger at Bé and said, "It's high time that thing comes to help me sell. It's old enough. What use is it at home?"

Bé slinked into the corner. Being in a stall with Big Mother all day sounded like a nightmare come to life.

"She is needed here to watch the house and guard the property. Someone must do it, now that my mother is gone," Ba said.

Bé stopped breathing as she listened to the conversation.

"We have dogs for that," Big Mother said. "And what can a mute do when the robbers come?"

"Robbers will not dare if there is someone here," Ba said. "You are needed at the market. The boys are needed to help in the fields. And my daughter is of use here."

Though Big Mother never listened to Ba, she begrudgingly accepted the truth in his words and let the matter drop. Relief fluttered through Bé. Safe for a little while longer.

When night came and the last wisps of sunlight disappeared, Bé shut all the windows and doors of the main house tightly. It was safe during the day, when South Vietnamese soldiers patrolled the area, but once it got dark, the soldiers were pulled away to the battlefield. Some nights, they had no soldiers protecting them, and that's when it was the most dangerous—when the Việt Cộng came down from the mountains.

"They want to scare and intimidate us, and there is

nothing we can do but pray our troops win the war," a neighbor had once warned them.

Bé's brothers loved to scare her with stories about the Việt Cộng. "They'll burn an arm here, chop off a leg there." Bảo had cackled. "They'll hang you upside down over a spit and let a nest of fire ants eat you up."

Bé may have been eleven years old, old enough to know the stories were meant to taunt her, but they still scared Bé enough to keep her from running away, no matter how badly her stepmother treated her. Big Mother's wrath was nothing compared to the Việt Cộng.

*When I grow up, Ba will arrange for me to marry a good husband from a nice family,* Bé reminded herself. *He'll make sure they are nice and nothing like Big Mother.*

Once married, Bé would have to live with her husband's family, as was the custom, but she trusted her father. Most girls were married off at eighteen.

*Only seven more years if Má doesn't come back.* Bé balled her hands into fists. *No, she will come back for me. She promised.*

Since the war had become more dangerous, the family gathered at night in the largest room in the house.

There, the ancestral altar sat on display, surrounded by burned incense sticks in a porcelain pot, and framed black-and-white photographs of Ba's parents and his paternal grandparents. A large bowl of fresh fruit sat in the center of the altar, an offering to the ancestors. Sometimes when Bé was very hungry and no was looking, she would light some incense sticks, say her silent apology to her ancestors, and swipe an orange or a mango from the altar.

*Sorry, Bà Nội. Tell the ancestors to forgive me*, she'd silently pray.

The room had no windows, but during the day, four sets of wooden double doors opened to bring in the sunlight. A table and set of chairs were next to the altar for when the family had guests. The hammock where Ba slept hung in the corner.

Big Mother lit a small kerosene lamp with just enough light to see, but not enough that anyone outside could tell that the house was occupied. They stayed quiet and in darkness because they didn't want the Việt Cộng to know they were there.

The only sound in the room was the swish of Big

Mother's silk and bamboo hand fan as she fanned herself slowly. The rest of the family sweated.

There was safety in the dark, though. Big Mother couldn't punish Bé during these hours, too afraid of the noise. Bé fingered the rosary, hidden in her pocket. *A prayer for the impossible to come true*, Cha had said.

Bé prayed for Mèo and the other kittens. Bé prayed that Big Mother would leave her alone. But most of all, Bé prayed for Má to come back.

The dogs guarding the property began to bark, emitting short, low-pitched growls. Everyone froze. The family waited and listened. Was it a stray animal, or the Việt Cộng?

The dogs quieted down and everyone let out a collective breath. Ba sat next to Bé and grabbed her hand. Bé felt the poison in Big Mother's glower from across the room.

"I love you best," Ba whispered in her ear. She leaned into him, basking in the love radiating from his skeletal body.

Across the dim room, Xuân was playing con quay— spinning tops—with his brothers. This was his favorite game—one he could play in pitch dark, one he used to play with Bé.

Bé looked away, feeling again for the rosary in her pocket.

Later that night, Bé lay on the floor of the bedroom she shared with her brothers. The concrete floor felt cool against her back, but the heat and humidity in the small room were stifling. She stared at the bamboo mats, soft pillows, and blue mosquito netting on her brothers' beds.

Bé turned this way and that, trying to get comfortable, but the floor was hard and jabbed into her bony back. She missed the nights when Má had fanned her to sleep in comfort on their plush bed.

She slapped her arm, killing a mosquito. She had no mosquito net protecting her, and the itchy bites on her arms and legs kept her wide awake. Bé scratched until she bled. Bé thought about how carefully Má had used to tuck the mosquito net underneath their mattress. No bugs had ever bit her then. *Does Má sleep well? Does she have a net?*

Without her mother, all Bé had for comfort was her small, tattered pillow. No one touched her pillow; they thought it was full of mites and bedbugs. If there were bugs inside her pillow, they didn't bother her.

Her brothers snored like a cacophony of snorting wild boars, deep and low. Outside, Bé heard the faint sound of machine guns and explosions in the distance. Any day now, the war would be at their door.

Bé removed the rosary from her pocket. She clutched the beads and hoped for the impossible that her mother was safe.

The beads were smooth and hard in her fingers, and the metal cross was sharp at the ends. She looped it around her neck and wore it as a necklace. She pretended that she was a rich royal princess of old, like in the scroll paintings that hung in Big Mother's room, and the bedtime stories her mother used to tell her.

If she were the crown princess, she'd have long hair again, not this short, jagged hair that Big Mother cut whenever she pleased. How she missed her hair. As a princess, her hair would always be perfectly brushed, not one strand out of place. And sometimes, she'd keep her hair up in a perfect bun with the most delicate ivory chopsticks going through it. She'd always be clean and smell of soap and night blooming jasmine. And the áo dài dress she'd wear would be made of the finest silk and embroidered with fine gold. A delicate umbrella would shield her unblemished skin from the sun. She would be cherished and beloved by all. No one would ever hurt her. Má would be right next to her, holding her hand. They'd have two fluffy lion dogs following them wherever they'd go.

Bé dreamed of the imperial palace. During the day, they would sit on thrones with ornate headdresses made of pure gold. At night, they would sleep in a plush canopy bed, draped in silks and chiffons. Soft feathers would cradle her off to a heavenly slumber.

Her dreams carried her away.

Princess Bé was sitting at a table piled high with her favorite fruit, pastries, and desserts when an explosion of stars filled her vision, and a painful slap to her bruised cheek pulled her awake.

Bé opened her eyes.

Big Mother's face was inches from her own. Her stepmother's eyes were bloodshot, eyebrows severely slanted sharply down, like she was about to have a stroke.

Bé wished she would.

"You little thief!" Big Mother pulled Bé up by her shirt. The girl blinked, her eyes adjusting to the bright early morning light. She squirmed and kicked, trying to get out of her stepmother's grasp.

"Where did you get this?!"

# CHAPTER 13

*THE ROSARY*. Bé began to panic.

Big Mother pulled at the string of beads around Bé's neck. "You stole it from the church, I know you did! A thief, just like your concubine mother!"

Big Mother jerked at the rosary, and the string that held the necklace together snapped. Bé watched in horror as the string of beads fell to the ground and Big Mother stomped on them, smashing them under her hefty weight.

Bé wanted to scream. She tried to wriggle away from Big Mother. She wanted to save some of the beads, but the woman didn't let go.

Cha had trusted her to keep the rosary safe, and she had failed. She had broken her promise.

"You think you're so holy, don't you? You want to be Christian, do you? Like your worthless mother! When the rest of us are Buddhist!" Big Mother screamed. "Xuân, come here, son!"

Xuân, always the last one to wake in the mornings, was halfway out the door, trying to escape, but when he heard Big Mother's voice, all the muscles in his back tightened. The knots hardened on his lanky frame. When he turned, his face was as pale as ivory.

Bé kicked and thrashed around. Big Mother was as strong as a pig, and Bé was only skin and bones. Her struggle made her stepmother more furious.

"Hold her arms down behind her back. Don't let her escape," Big Mother commanded Xuân.

He stood there shaking his head, not obeying.

*Leave Xuân alone!* Bé thought and spat in Big Mother's face.

"You little devil!" Big Mother squeezed her chin tight. "You are unlovable and a nuisance. Like the flies that bite into your flesh. Flies that carry disease and death."

"XUÂN, COME HERE!" Big Mother screeched. "Or I'll make you wish you were never born."

Xuân avoided looking at his sister and followed his mother's instructions. His hands shook violently as he held Bé's arms.

*No, Xuân!* Bé wanted to cry. She could see the fear in Xuân's face. *Fight her, Xuân!* she silently yelled. Her brother would have never allowed this when they were little. A tear slipped from her eye.

Big Mother stomped over to a desk in the corner of the room and grabbed a bamboo reed quill filled with green ink. Bé shook, resisting, while her heart thundered in her ear. The bile in her stomach churned, threatening to come out.

"NO! MOTHER! DON'T!" Xuân choked out, but before Bé knew what was happening, Big Mother took hold of her head and began marking her forehead with the quill. The sharp tip scratched into her skin. Bé screamed, but no sound came out, only a croak.

"You are worthless, nothing but a thief. You will be marked forever by what you've stolen," Big Mother seethed.

Xuân sobbed, tears streaming down his face. He rubbed his thumb gently against his sister's hand, trying to comfort her. Bé felt only hate and anger course through her veins. She hated Big Mother. Hated her for taking away everything she had loved. She hated Xuân too. Hated him for being weak. Hated him for not standing up to his mother. Hated him for leaving her.

"He thought she was beautiful, like a lotus. A lotus! The flower of the dawn. He said he never loved me. He wanted a girl, and she gave him a daughter, and all that came from my womb were boys." Big Mother's words were hard and loud. She was lost in her tirade as the quill continued to scratch into Bé's forehead. Big Mother moved it left and right, up and down.

The pain overwhelmed Bé. Dark spots filled her eyes. Then Bé realized she was bleeding. Red droplets trickled down into her eyes and onto her cheeks.

Big Mother released her and said, "Steal again, and I'll hand you over to the Việt Cộng myself." Then she turned and stomped out.

Bé and Xuân both crumpled to the floor, shaking like the swaying trees during typhoon season. The wind thrashed, and they were uprooted.

"I am so sorry, Little Sister. I—I . . . I should have

tried to stop it." Xuân sobbed. "I didn't know . . . I didn't know."

Bé couldn't hear him. She was broken, like the shards of green glass that surrounded her. Her tears wouldn't stop coming, and she heaved from her pain. Her forehead throbbed.

"M-m-m-m-á-á-á," she managed to croak out, curling into a ball. The sound was garbled and unintelligible.

Xuân disappeared to find Ba. It felt like forever before her father found her, shaking and whimpering soundlessly in a ball. How much time had passed, how many tears, how many drops of blood, she didn't know. Heart aching, she had escaped further into herself, looking for comfort within her memories.

Ba placed a steaming plate of chả giò—fried spring roll—on the ground. Untangling his daughter's arms and legs from her body, he cupped her face in his. Bé couldn't stand seeing the horror and pity in his face, so she eyed the chả giò, grabbed one, and shoved it into her mouth. She focused on the soothing comfort of the warm meat filling as it slid down her hungry belly, calming her. She took another one, and then another.

The dried blood on her face cracked, the wound on her forehead throbbing. She gorged herself on the food.

"Easy, now," said Ba.

He wiped the remaining blood off her face with his sleeve, careful not to touch the wound. Her father's face remained solemn; the crow's feet around his eyes looked more wrinkled, and the frown lines around his mouth deepened. He got up and returned several minutes later, carrying a warm bowl of water and a soft cloth. With the wet cloth, he cleaned his daughter's wound carefully.

"You're safe. Everything will be all right. She's gone to the market now," Ba said. He wrapped his skeletal arms around her and rocked her back and forth like he did when she was a young girl and woke up from terrible nightmares.

She wanted to never let him go. She wanted to bury her face in his arms and stay there forever.

"Thương Thương, my love," Ba said, and she warmed at the sound of her true name. "I'm a feeble old man now, powerless to protect you, unable to keep your mother . . . I . . . I have failed you. I should have sent you away sooner, but I didn't want to be without you, but now . . . now I must."

Bé gently wriggled from his embrace and shook her head. *No. No. Ba, you can't send me away!*

Panic replaced her tears. How would Má find her if he sent her away?

That afternoon, Bé gathered up the broken bits of the rosary. Using a needle and thread, she sewed the remnants into the hem of her favorite shirt—a light blue, long-sleeved tunic that buttoned in the middle. It had been Má's, and Bé had saved it from being burned in the bonfire. Bé removed her worn brown shirt and draped the blue one over her head. It was loose on Bé, but the fabric was soft and allowed the breeze to flow through it, cooling her on hot days.

Bé prayed for the impossible and plotted to stay with Ba, no matter what.

# CHAPTER 14

Bé's forehead healed slowly in the weeks that followed. She often picked at the scab, using her nails to dig into the wound, desperately wanting to get rid of the ink. It was useless. A green ink tattoo remained, etched into the shape of a cross. Green, the color of jealousy and lust, and the cross, a symbol showing that she was different from her family. Bé first tried to use her bangs to cover her mutilated forehead, but Big Mother just cut them shorter, wanting the world to see.

*What would Má think if she saw me now?* Bé wondered. *She probably wouldn't recognize me with a scar and choppy, dirty hair.* Bé had stopped washing her hair since soapy water irritated her wound. She didn't have a comb or brush—they had been burned in the bonfire—so Bé's hair was unkempt most of the time. *Would Má be ashamed?*

Big Mother's eyes gleamed whenever she looked at Bé. Xuân avoided her, and Ba looked defeated, shoulders always hunched. Bé tried not to think about that. Instead, she was diligent about getting all her chores done. She wanted Ba to see what a great help she was, and how necessary she was to the running of their home. Ba did seem pleased, but Bé was still fearful that Ba would stay true to his promise to send her away.

One month after that nightmarish day, Bé climbed up high in her tamarind tree to spy on her father. Bé looked up to the sky to try to predict the weather. It was the beginning of monsoon season, and the sky was overcast, but there were no ominous clouds forming. She had time to spy.

For the past week, Ba had been secretly meeting with strangers out in the street, just out of Bé's earshot. His meetings were always timed just right—Big Mother was away at the market, and the boys were taking their afternoon naps. Bé couldn't hear the conversation, but she knew her father seemed dejected after they walked away. That gave her hope.

She peered out between the leaves and spotted him with Cha, the kind priest who had given her the rosary. The two men spoke in hushed tones, standing very close to each other. They walked away in the direction of the church. *What were they talking about?*

Bé stayed in her tree for a long time, picking ripe tamarind and eating its sweet flesh. She loved hearing the crack of the hard shell and chewing the brown-colored sticky fruit on the inside. She spat out the large black seed, watching it drop below. She continued to eat until her belly was full, then selected a handful of the fruit and put it in her pocket to save for later. When Ba and Cha were no longer in sight, she climbed down, slipped on her sandals, and went about her chores.

As Bé scattered feed for the chickens, her thoughts raced about her father meeting with Cha. *If Ba keeps his promise, where will he send me? Didn't Cha say Má was an orphan? Doesn't that mean she has no family? Maybe Ba will try to find us a place to live together. Or maybe he's trying to find Má, and when he finds her, he'll send me*

*to live with her! Cha said Má saw him before she left . . .*
*Maybe he knows where she is.*

"Mew! Mew! Mew!" The squeaky meowing coming from inside the hay mound distracted Bé from her thoughts. It was frantic and becoming louder with each second that passed.

Bé dropped her basket of chicken feed, sending the chickens around her clucking and flapping their wings unhappily at the interruption. Bé ignored them. She ran to the mound and pushed aside the hay to uncover her cat family's den.

They were gone.

Clumps of matted fur and what looked like blood on the ground were all that remained of Bà Già's family. Tears pricked the edges of Bé's vision—she couldn't lose Bà Già too, after everything that had happened.

Then she heard the mewing again. It was one of the baby kittens.

It was louder, closer, deeper within.

Bé dove into the mound, pushing hay out of her way, following the sound of mewing. Loose hay covered her from top to bottom, and beneath a matted clump, Bé soon found Mèo, the tiny runt of the litter with the gray striped fur. He was missing a front paw, and it looked like something, maybe a dog, had gotten a good bite out of him. He mewed in pain. Bé gingerly picked up the baby kitten and cuddled him.

The pads of Mèo's remaining paws felt cold, so Bé held him even closer to her body. The kitten purred in response to Bé's petting.

Bé quickly looked around the chicken enclosure for Bà Già and the other kittens, but they were nowhere to be found. She hoped against impossible hope that they had survived and were safe in another hiding spot. Bé's chest felt tight, but Mèo purred in her arms, and when she gazed into his round, yearning eyes, she felt comforted. Mèo nipped at her finger with his tiny teeth and Bé silently giggled. It tickled.

Mèo's missing paw oozed a small drop of blood onto Bé's shirt, so she ran toward the well by the house with her kitten cuddled close. There, she found Xuân home early. They had been avoiding each other since that terrible day. He looked at her, opened his mouth to say something, then promptly closed his mouth again. He swallowed hard. Bé stared back, feeling awkward.

Xuân's gaze fell onto the bundle in Bé's hands.

Bé bit her lip, not sure if she could trust him. The kitten purred in her hands, and Bé saw the somber expression on her brother's face, so she decided to risk it. She opened her hands and showed him Mèo.

Xuân looked at her for a long moment and said, "You have to hide him from my mother. She will eat that cat if she finds it or sell it to someone who will."

Bé scowled at Xuân's response. But then she nodded. She knew. The siblings had kept Bà Già a secret because of this.

In the village, no one kept house cats, because they brought in fleas and bugs. And some of the poorer, hungrier people in the village would eat any meat they could find. The year before, one of Ba's dogs had gone missing, and they'd learned a thief had dognapped it and sold it to someone as meat. People also went to Monkey Hill to hunt monkeys for food. Others ate cat meat as well, thinking that boiled cat meat would cure diseases.

Mèo shivered in Bé's arms, and she held him close to her face. *I won't let anything happen to you*, she thought. This kitten didn't have a mother anymore, just like Bé.

"We'll need to clean his paw," Xuân said after a moment.

Xuân drew water from their well, and together they washed Mèo's injured leg. He meowed and nipped at them in protest. Bé went inside the house and tore a strip of cloth from her tattered pillow cover for them to use. Xuân bandaged Mèo's paw while Bé held him close. Mèo licked her face, his sandpaper tongue tickling Bé's skin, and she smiled.

Afterward, Xuân ran to the neighbor's house to buy a bowl of rice porridge for the kitten. When he returned, he emptied half of the plastic bag of rice porridge into a shallow bowl for Mèo and poured the rest into a bowl for Bé.

"Peace offering?" he asked a little hesitantly.

Bé considered this for a few moments, and then slowly nodded her head. She dug into her pocket and handed him a ripe tamarind pod.

Xuân hugged her then, pulling her in so tight that Bé squeaked in surprise. She hugged him back, and it was as if the invisible wall that had separated them for almost two years melted away.

"What should we call him?" Xuân asked as he finished his last bit of tamarind.

Mèo meowed at that very moment, and Xuân laughed. Bé had missed hearing his laugh.

The kitten meowed again, and Bé nodded at Xuân with a smile.

"Mèo?" Xuân asked.

Bé nodded again. *Mèo.*

The days that followed were peaceful. Ba went back to his old routine—no more secret meetings in the street. *He must see that Big Mother and I are getting along now*, Be thought. *He won't send me away.*

Bé sewed a large chest pocket inside her favorite shirt, the one with the rosary hidden in its hem, for Mèo to sleep in. She wore the shirt most days, taking it off only to wash whenever it got too dirty or smelly. The kitten's injured paw healed fast and, before long, he walked without any trouble. *His three-legged hop is the cutest*, Bé thought, watching him play about.

Xuân helped keep Mèo a secret from Big Mother. He snuck the kitten bits of his food, and when Bé cleared away the family's food plates after meals, she picked off any fish meat left on the bones and saved them for her kitten. When it rained and they brought Mèo inside, Xuân distracted his brothers when they thought they saw movement in the corners of the room, telling them that their eyes were playing tricks on them—it was just the shadows, or a field mouse had gotten inside, and they'd never catch it even if they tried. At night, when the family huddled together in the ancestral room, Xuân hid Mèo in a closet. Only when everyone else had gone to sleep did Bé come to get him. Mèo always knew Bé was coming and head bumped the girl's leg, purring.

During the day, after Big Mother left for the market, Bé let Mèo roam around. Mèo followed Bé everywhere. When she was sweeping the outdoor kitchen, Mèo tried to nibble on the leftover food remnants on the ground. When Bé burned the trash in the backyard, the gray striped kitten kept watch a little farther away, licking his paws and stretching out as they waited for the trash to burn fully. Mèo climbed up Bé's leg when they got close to the pigsty, or when the dogs chained up outside growled at him. Bé would then place him in his special pocket and continue the rest of the chores. The warmth from Mèo's body comforted Bé.

Sometimes Bé and Mèo would sit and watch the monsoon rain from the ancestral room, and Mèo kept her company as she folded clothes and cleaned the house. Mèo loved swatting at bugs and finding the most random objects that had been dropped behind cabinets and bookcases. Once he killed a tiny mouse in the kitchen.

Every afternoon when Xuân returned home, he found excuses to sneak away. On dry days, Bé and Xuân hid behind the hay mound and played with Mèo. He ran up and down their bodies like they were trees and made for climbing. Once a giggle nearly escaped Bé. Her voice ached to return, but still no sound left her lips. On rainy days, they'd play with Mèo in Bà Nội's old room, now abandoned and used for storage, away from their other brothers' prying eyes.

It felt like old times, and Bé was happy in these moments with her brother and Mèo.

## CHAPTER 15

PEACEFUL DAYS turned to blissful weeks. It was dry out and the sun was peeking behind the clouds on the horizon. Bé chased Mèo around the chicken enclosure as they waited for Xuân. Bé imagined Ma's voice singing in the wind, as the lightest of breezes danced on her skin. Mèo ran up her leg and onto her chest. She twirled him around and then hugged him to her.

"Bé!" Big Mother called in the distance.

Her voice made Bé jump. She was home early. Too early. And she called her "Bé," not "it" or "devil." All the hairs on Bé's arms rose.

Big Mother called for her again.

Since Bé was wearing her favorite shirt, she slid Mèo

in her pocket and looked around, trying to decide where to hide the kitten so she could go to Big Mother.

All of a sudden the chickens let out frenzied squawks, flapping their wings and running all over the place, and a man jumped out of the shadows. Bé stumbled backward.

"Such a pretty girl," he snarled.

Bé had never seen the man before. He was heavyset with oily black hair, a bulbous nose, and a crooked grin on his face. Black teeth poked out underneath his lips, and in one of his hands, he held a burlap sack.

Even before he lunged for her, Bé knew she was in trouble. Bé stumbled over an escaping chicken, and the man easily caught her in his arms. His skin was slick with sweat, and he reeked of cigarettes and hog manure. His breath smelled foul too, like he'd let dried squid ferment in his mouth.

*Get off me!* She silently yelled, pulling hard against his grip. When that didn't work, she kneed him in the groin. She took off, legs pumping, hair flying, racing faster and faster. She thought of Xuân and how they used to race in the paddy fields. She wished her brother were there now, but she was glad he had always made her race.

She heard the man swear loudly, calling for her to stop, his heavy footsteps clomping hard on the dirt behind her.

Mèo stirred, but Bé held her hand over her chest, keeping Mèo in place. She ran faster, but her legs were starting to ache. She looked back, and the man was right on her heels, not far away now.

Big Mother waved for Bé from the terrace. For the first time in her life, she was thankful to see her. She ran through the courtyard and reached her stepmother.

Bé stopped, panting, trying to catch her breath.

Safety.

Any minute now, Big Mother would yell at the strange man to get off their property. But Big Mother did not yell at the man, who had come to an abrupt stop only five feet away from them. Instead, Big Mother pulled Bé to her and said, "One of my nephews has found your mother."

Before Bé could gather her thoughts, a damp burlap sack was thrown over her body and she choked, inhaling sweet-smelling fumes. She instinctively threw her hands up, trying to force the sack off. Big Mother's meaty hands held the sack over Bé as she struggled.

*Stop! What's happening? Why are you doing this? BA!* Bé searched for a scream inside her.

Bé felt the coarse burlap fabric press against her face, and she kicked with all her might. The powerful scent of hog manure overwhelmed Bé. She gagged and inhaled more of the fumes. She felt Mèo's small body go limp inside her secret pocket. The poisonous fumes had knocked him out.

Bé lost feeling in her arms and legs, but she kept wiggling, kept fighting. Her sandals slipped off her feet. She couldn't breathe. She needed air.

*XUÂN! BA!* She tried to scream, but nothing came out, only the sound of gasping. Her arms and legs felt heavy. *Why can't I move my legs? What is happening to me?*

"Fifty thousand đồng," Big Mother said. "The money we agreed on."

The man grunted and said, "They'll pay you double. Tomorrow. At your stall."

*Why are they paying her money? Where are they*

*taking me?* Bé's head throbbed, and her vision narrowed at the edges. The darkness spread inward.

"She is mute, and very obedient. You will have no trouble with her," Big Mother said. "Now take her, and don't let anyone see you."

Bé struggled to keep her consciousness, the light only a pinhole in her vision. She felt the arms of someone picking her up. She heard the distant revving of a motor-bike and Big Mother's voice saying, "Good riddance."

The motorbike shook underneath her. Then all went black.

PART 3

# OUT OF THE DARKNESS, A GLIMMER

# CHAPTER 16

Metallic clanging. Loud banging. Someone crying. The scatter of feet on the ground. Whispers all around.

Someone brushed Bé's hair while someone else wiped her face with something rough and damp. She felt water on her chapped lips. She parted them and let the liquid in. Her throat was so dry. It felt like she had been without water for weeks, but she hadn't . . . had she?

Bé's eyelids felt glued shut. Her head was too heavy to lift, like a huge pig was sitting on top of her body. A young girl giggled.

Bé let sleep take her again.

When Bé opened her eyes, she saw nothing but inky blackness. The color of monsters and nightmares. She heard hushed whispers—voices speaking all around her, but she saw nothing except the dark. She blinked, but her eyes wouldn't focus. *Am I dead?*

Her throat was raw and tasted metallic. Her head throbbed, as if an imaginary giant were squeezing her brain to mush. The air felt damp and cool, smelling strongly of mold and human waste. Bé shivered.

Something clattered to the ground, followed by a splash.

"You're finally awake!" said a young girl's voice.

The room was eerily quiet, except for the shifting sounds of moving fabric. Dark shadows moved around her. She couldn't make out any features, only shapes. Too many shapes leaned toward her.

*This isn't happening.* Bé scooted backward from the shapes and ran into a wall—a mud wall. It stuck to her back, cool and wet like the ground during the rainy season.

She thought of the scary stories her mother used to tell her when she misbehaved, stories about monsters and shadow creatures outside her window that waited to eat naughty children. She thought about spirits conjured by black magic, translucent beings some people claimed to see at night. *Are these shadows and shapes real? Are they out to steal my soul?*

Bé looked for safety in better memories, like when she was younger and slept peacefully between Má and Ba. Bé shut her eyes. *Maybe I'm dreaming, and when I wake, I'll be in the bedroom with my brothers.* She wanted to be anywhere but there.

After a few moments, Bé forced herself to open her eyes.

She blinked. This was real.

The shapes and shadows were real.

*I have to get out of here!*

Bé dug her nails into the mud wall and forced her shaking legs to stand. *Where was the door?* She looked around but saw nothing but blackness. She turned left and ran straight into another wall. *What is this place? Why can't I see?*

Suddenly, she couldn't breathe, couldn't get enough air. She felt trapped, caged.

A hand touched her leg, and she jumped and fell on top of someone.

"Ow! Watch it!" said an angry voice. A woman's voice.

Bé scampered off her and bumped into someone else. *Why are there so many people in here? Are they all prey for the shadow monster? Or worse?*

"Shhhh, you're all right. You're just in shock," said a calmer, gentler voice. She guided Bé back to the ground. "It'll take some time for the poison to wear off."

*Poison.*

Bé repeated the word in her head over and over again. *Poison. Poisoned.* She had been poisoned.

*What happened?* Bé closed her eyes and tried to remember. But her brain was foggy like the lingering smoke that surrounded a trash fire, clouding everything around. She vaguely remembered a chase, a man who smelled of cigarettes and hog manure . . . The revving of a motorbike . . .

Then the air was knocked from her lungs and Bé remembered.

Big Mother.

She had tricked her and allowed the stranger to drug and kidnap her. For fifty thousand đồng.

Big Mother had sold her.

Bé wanted to throw up.

She pulled her knees to her chest. Suddenly, her teeth chattered, and she was freezing, so very cold, though sweat dripped down her face and back. *Is this the lingering effect of the fumes?* A tingling sensation crept its way through her spine and into her fingers, prickling like she had bugs crawling underneath her skin.

"It was bad for me when I got here, too," said the young girl's voice. "I was shaking so hard that I threw up, and I kept throwing up."

*Where is "here"?*

*Where am I?*

Bé heard a dunk, water splashing, and then someone handed her something—a metal cup that felt cool against her hands. Hands helped guide it to her mouth, and she drank. The water tasted gritty and metallic, not clean like the water from the well at home, but it felt good going down. She drank it fast, and then wanted more. She hadn't realized how thirsty she was. The cup was taken away and refilled, and Bé gulped more down.

"Sometimes the men mess up on the dose, and they're dead when they drag them in here." It was the girl's voice again.

*Dead.* Bé shuddered at the word, imagining corpses surrounding her, blue and cold and left to rot in this place. *Is this place a grave? How many people have died here?*

"Ngân, don't scare her like that," said the gentle-voiced woman. Bé felt arms wrap around her, and she froze. The last time anyone had touched her had been Big Mother and the man on the motorbike.

"Let her speak the truth. No point in lying about it," growled an angry voice. The woman Bé had tripped over. "Death is better than a life you can't ever escape. You can try and try, but no one escapes this hell. They all end up dead, dead, dead."

*No escape? Dead?*

Bé swallowed hard. *Will I be trapped here in the dark forever? Will I die here? Will they kill me? Whoever they are?* She didn't have a lot of experience with death.

She'd only seen one dead body before, and that was her Bà Nội.

Bé didn't want to think about her grandmother's corpse, how limp and lifeless she had looked the day they buried her. She didn't want to remember how deep and dark that hole was. She felt trapped in the dark, just like Bà Nội.

The shadows moved, and Bé forced herself to breathe, to be calm, to shrink back into the wall.

Finally, Bé's eyes began to adjust to the darkness. She could make out more detail in the shapes. Many women, all thin and fragile, huddled together on the ground in a small space—about the size of the bedroom she used to share with her mother. They wore loose buttoned-up shirts and dark pants that were too big for their tiny frames.

The walls were mud and the ground a smooth tile. There was no window, and Bé couldn't see a door, though there had to be one, and she was determined to find it. The women leaned away from one corner of the room, where Bé could make out the outline of a bucket. Misery and sorrow emanated from everyone.

Bé wanted to pinch her nose; the entire room reeked of urine and human waste, and the smell became worse and worse the longer she was awake.

Bé wrapped her arms around herself, feeling the soft fabric of her favorite shirt. She put her hand in the pocket she had sewn for Mèo.

*Mèo!* The wet prickle of tears formed in the corner of her eyes. *Where is he? Had he been left back at home? Was he safe?*

Bé clutched the hem of her shirt, where she had sewn the broken rosary, and she prayed to any god that might exist to take her home or take her to her mother. Cha had said it was a necklace of hope and prayer for the impossible to come true. She needed hope now more than ever before.

# CHAPTER 17

Soft fur bumped against Bé's legs, followed by a familiar mew.

*Mèo?*

A kitten jumped on top of her knees and began to purr. It felt like Mèo and smelled like Mèo.

Tears burst from Bé's eyes as she squeezed her beloved kitten in disbelief. She kissed him all over, and Mèo purred in response. For a second, Bé forgot everything. She forgot about this scary, dark place and the shadows and women around her. In that second, she and Mèo were outside, running around the chicken enclosure, playing with Xuân.

*Xuân.*

She and Mèo had been waiting for him when they were taken. *Is he worried about me?* Bé wondered what lie Big Mother had told Xuân and Ba. *Did she tell them I ran away? Would they believe her? Would they come looking for me?* She hoped Xuân would. Maybe he was out in their neighborhood, yelling her name. Maybe he and Ba would go find Cha and form a rescue party. Maybe they were trying to find her at this very moment. Maybe they would succeed and save her from this place.

Bé's heart ached for Xuân. She'd lost him, just when she'd finally gotten him back. She gave Mèo another big squeeze. He was all she had left in the world.

"You were out for hours. We thought you were dead, and your kitten kept trying to lick you awake," said Ngân, the young girl.

Although Bé couldn't see her well in the dark, she could tell that Ngân was a thin stick of a girl, her clothes oversized for her skinny frame. She looked sickly, but her voice was strong.

"We're happy we have something to kill the rats," said the angry-voiced woman.

*Rats?* Bé's skin itched, and she imagined a nest of black rats crawling up her body into her hair, biting her with their little teeth. She shuddered.

"How old are you?" asked Ngân, pulling Bé out of her thoughts.

*Should I trust her?* Bé didn't know, but it was an innocent question and she decided to answer.

Bé grabbed the girl's hand and turned it over so that her palm faced up. She tapped her palm eleven times.

"I'm thirteen, only two years older than you," said Ngân.

*This girl seems friendly*, Bé thought, and it helped her feel a little better.

"You are too young," murmured Cô Lan, the gentle-voiced woman. "You don't even have your monthlies yet." She tsked.

Bé didn't know what monthlies were, and as the group of women talked, Bé stared blankly and tried to make sense of it all.

"I don't have mine yet, but Cô Lan says it's coming soon," Ngân said.

"I didn't get one until I was fifteen," said another

voice. "But my village was very poor, and no one ever got enough to eat."

"It's a curse down here. They don't ever remove the rags, and we're having to wash and reuse the same one over and over, month after month," the angry woman said.

*What is she talking about? What curse? What rags? Do all these women have a disease? Will I get sick with it too?* Bé had too many questions and no answers.

"They're kidnapping them younger and younger," butted in yet another woman.

As Bé listened, she wondered if by some miracle Má was there. Bé strained her ear for Má's familiar voice in the crowd . . . but she didn't hear it. She didn't know whether to be disappointed or glad. She desperately wanted to find her mother.

"Our grown bodies can't keep up with the demand," snapped the angry woman.

*What does "grown bodies can't keep up with the demand" mean? Are the monsters that had caged them working them to death?* Work did not scare Bé. She had spent the last two years working every single day, and she was used to strenuous labor.

"What's your name?" asked Ngân.

When Bé didn't answer, she asked, "Can you talk? Do you still have your tongue?"

Bé looked at her curiously and then stuck out her tongue. Of course she still had a tongue. Just because she didn't talk didn't mean she didn't have a tongue.

Ngân stuck her tongue back, and then laughed like a carefree girl. Laughter felt out of place here, but it helped ease a little of Bé's fear. It was strange to have light and joy in such a terrifying place.

Ngân leaned in close and whispered, "Tuyết, over there in the corner. They cut out her tongue. I heard the men say it's because she couldn't stop screaming when she was aboveground. Now she cries and cries and makes grunting noises in her sleep."

*What men? Aboveground? Were they buried underground?* The thought squeezed the air from Bé's lungs. *Did they do something to make her scream so much? Or had she gone mad?* Bé had never met anyone who'd lost their mind, but she'd heard Big Mother gossip plenty about people who had and the danger they posed in the market, especially during a war. No one ever knew if they'd bring in a bomb, or if they'd steal.

"Everyone thought she was going to die. We tried our best to nurse her. She didn't die, but now she moans and grunts. The men take her up a lot more now."

"Ngân," warned Cô Lan.

Bé rubbed her temples. Her head was throbbing. Would she end up like Tuyết? Is this what happened if you stayed here too long?

Bé wanted to go home. She wished she could climb her tamarind tree and hide. She wished she could hide behind the hay mound.

But there was nowhere to hide.

She clutched Mèo closer to her. His sandpaper tongue licked her nose before he wriggled out of her grasp to settle onto her lap.

"Rest now," soothed Cô Lan. "You'll feel better in the morning." She wrapped her arms around Bé. This time, Bé let her, grabbing her arm like it was the only thing keeping her from drowning. She was like a mountain fairy from the fables Má used to tell her, and this lady's arm was the end of a fisherman's hook, pulling her up from the depths of the ocean. Cô Lan's warmth reminded Bé of Má, and how close Má used to hold her when she woke up from a nightmare. Má would say, "It's not real. You're safe. I'm here."

The thought of being trapped in this underground box forever, where Má could never find her, pulled Bé down, down, down, like rocks in her stomach drowning her in the sea. The air was sucked out of the room, sucked out of her lungs. Her head was underwater. She was sinking, sinking, sinking.

Ngân leaned and hugged her too. Mèo purred and butted his head against Bé's stomach. He licked her hand, as if telling Bé that everything would be all right.

But she knew. Everything was not all right.

# CHAPTER 18

Bé WOKE with a start. The stale, suffocating air reeked even more. Bé could taste the odor of human waste on her tongue. Sweat dotted her forehead from the heat of the room, and her heart hammered like a stampede of water buffalo. She was caged like the monkey at her great-uncle's house, but at least now she wasn't in the dark. It was morning, and the cramped, windowless room was illuminated by a single light bulb on the low ceiling, and rays of light radiated from underneath a solid iron door.

*A door!*

Tongueless Tuyết was banging her fists on it, sobbing. She pounded and pounded. Her mournful cries and unintelligible groans reminded Bé of the whimpering of a dog wanting out of its kennel.

The banging scared Mèo. He mewed pitifully and hid behind Bé, like a turtle withdrawing inside its shell.

"Will you stop it, Tuyết? You're giving me a migraine. No one is coming!" yelled the angry woman, who was fanning herself with a paper hand fan. In the night, Bé had learned her name—Cô Bích—along with the names of a few others.

Bé ran to the door, stepping over the bodies of women still sleeping on the faded blue-tiled ground. Tuyết ignored her and kept banging. Bé ran her hands over the smooth iron. *Where is the doorknob?*

The light in the room was still dim, but not the pitch-blackness of last night. The amount of light reminded Bé of how the ancestral room looked in the evenings when the family burned the small kerosene lamp.

Bé could finally make out the features of her roommates. Ngân was much thinner than she was, only skin and bones, and slightly taller than Bé by half a head. Her long, matted black hair stuck to her face and shoulders, and her eyes sank into her face, her lips thin, cheeks hollow.

Cô Lan, who had held her in the night, looked about Má's age with high cheekbones and a loose braid on one side that pooled down at her hip. She was thin but bony. From the shape of her face, Bé could tell that it used to be round and full. *She must have been beautiful when she was well-fed and free*, Bé thought.

Cô Bích looked withered, like an old tree, with short hair and a long face. Her eyes were hard and full of fury. Her anger wasn't like Big Mother's though. Bé thought Cô Bích still had kindness in her heart. Last night, Cô Bích had covered a shivering Bé with a scratchy blanket to help her sleep.

Tuyết stopped banging. She sat by the door, shrieking incoherently and pulling her hair hard. She looked delirious, eyes wide and showing teeth like a rabid dog. Bé dared to touch her, wishing there was something she could do to stop her tantrum, but Tuyết flinched away.

Bé counted all the women in the room. There were twenty, and there was barely enough space for everyone to lie down. They were sweaty, clothes sticking to their bodies. The air was much warmer and more humid in the daytime.

Bé moved about the room, peering at the face of each woman, making absolutely sure none of them were Má. She wondered how long the women had been there. Some stared back at her with hollow, dead eyes. Others turned away, their eyes unfocused like they were barely hanging onto reality. Some turned their faces to the wall, whimpering and sobbing. A few women looked at Bé with sympathy.

*Má isn't here.*

Bé slumped against a mud wall. She wanted Má and Ba. She wanted Xuân. She wanted Bà Nội. She thought about Xuân's hug the day she had found Mèo injured, and she held onto that memory, letting the image fill her mind until she blocked out everything around her. That had been only weeks ago, when her life had been so very different.

Mèo jumped on her lap, as if sensing her sadness. He purred and Bé squeezed him like he was a stuffed animal. His soft fur was a sharp contrast to the hardness of the place. He trilled a high-pitch chirp, which made Bé smile. At least she still had her three-legged kitten. Mèo loved her. Bé kissed him all over. Her kitten made her feel less alone.

# CHAPTER 19

"IF YOU NEED to go, use the bucket in the corner," Ngan explained after she woke up. "They replace it every day with an empty one. Some days, it's so full that it splatters on the ground."

Bé made a face at that. No wonder the room reeked. Back at home, there was plenty of land where she could do her business. She'd dig a hole in the earth and cover it up when she was done. She never went in the same place twice.

"We get water here." Ngân motioned to a large pitcher of water that sat in the center of the room. A metallic cup sat on its lid. "A man comes once a day to bring us food and water."

*At least they feed them in the dungeon,* Bé thought.

"Who did that to you?" Ngân asked, reaching up to touch Bé's forehead.

Bé flinched away and hastily ruffled her short bangs to try and cover her scar.

"Does it hurt?" Ngân asked.

Bé shook her head and looked down. She didn't want to think about Big Mother or remember that terrible day.

She could feel Ngân still staring at her, but Ngân didn't say anything else.

"Do you know how to braid hair?" Ngân asked next. She wet her fingers and used them to comb out her hair.

Bé considered her question, then nodded slowly. Má had tried to teach Bé how to braid, but her fingers had been too small, and the sections of separated hair had become tangled in her fingers. But with no mirrors in the room, Ngân wouldn't know she wasn't good at it.

"I'll braid yours if you do mine. I want two braids."

Bé's hair wasn't long enough to braid, but she thought it was nice that Ngân offered.

Bé separated Ngân's hair into three sections and

began to work. She weaved the sections of hair together like Má had taught her, but the braid was fat and it stuck out in all the wrong places.

"Here, let me help you," said Cô Lan, and she placed her hands on Bé's. "You have to pull them tight like this, and you need to hide the shorter strands within the larger braid like so."

Together they worked to create two pretty braids, and Ngân smiled, pleased as she ran her fingers over them.

Bé's stomach began to growl, and so did Ngân's.

"We'll eat soon enough," Cô Lan said. To distract the girls, Cô Lan told them stories of her childhood, of her father's estate and the car they'd used to own. It had been the only car in the village, and everyone had been envious.

Bé hung onto Cô Lan's every word, and she imagined herself inside the shiny black automobile, looking out the window as the world passed, hearing the engine as it roared to life and carried her away.

Cô Lan fanned the girls with a paper fan as she spoke. Many of the other women had hand fans too.

"Wow. Your father was rich," Ngân said. "Like really,

really, really rich. People from my village only rode bicycles. We didn't have one though. We were too poor. We were lucky if we had enough money to buy rice to fill our bellies. Most days, we had to steal vegetables or fruit from our neighbors when they weren't home, or in the middle of the night when everyone was sleeping."

"I used to be very lucky," Cô Lan said. "I had everything I could ever want, and I threw it all away . . . I was a foolish, foolish girl."

"My village burned down, and my parents died. There was no one to take care of me. So my uncle drugged and sold me. He liked to bet in the neighbor's cockfights, and he was a winner at losing," Ngân said, her voice somber.

Bé frowned, feeling sad for her new friend. At least she had Ba and Xuân at home who loved her, and Má, too, wherever she was. And she had Mèo.

She scanned the room to find her kitten, who was busy getting pets from a group of women on the other side of the room. Mèo leaped from one woman's lap to the next, sitting down for a few minutes to let each woman pet him, before moving on. *He's a funny cat*, Bé thought. The women seemed delighted by his company.

Cô Lan said, "Everyone here was sold or kidnapped. All of us poisoned." She told the girls about her love who betrayed her. They had agreed to meet under the jackfruit tree near his grandparents' house and run away together. Her parents had been against the match, and they had arranged for her to marry someone else in the village. There had been rumors that her love was a Việt Cộng sympathizer, but she'd never believed them. She had completely trusted him, but he'd sold her to the traders. Under that jackfruit tree, he had tricked her with sweet words and a delicious, but poisonous, moon cake. She had been underground for a year, but even if she were freed, she could never go home. She had been chosen to go aboveground too often.

*What's aboveground? Why does everyone hate it? Why couldn't Cô Lan ever go home?* Bé hated not understanding.

"No one will marry me now," Cô Lan said.

*But why?* Bé wanted to ask.

"There is still hope for you girls. We hide Ngân when the men come at night. We take her place. We will do the same for you. We will find a way for you to escape," Cô Lan said.

"Escape?" cackled Cô Bích. "Lan, you deserve to be in a madhouse. No one ever escapes. Tuyết tried, I tried, but no one can even hear our screams. We are too far underground."

Bé shuddered at Cô Bích's words. She had fallen into that hole in the ground, buried, just like Bà Nội.

"I used to spend hours screaming, banging on the door when I first got here," said Cô Bích. "It's no good. Why care about us when there is a war and nasty men that need relieving."

*Men that need relieving?* Bé wondered what kind of job these men were doing that they needed women to replace them. *Are they making bombs for the war? Landmines?*

The door creaked open, just wide enough for a man to enter. He kicked the door closed behind him, but it didn't fully click shut.

Bé stared at the door. *Maybe, if I time it right . . . if I stand by the door when he opens it for mealtime . . . maybe I can sneak behind him. . . . Maybe I can escape.*

## CHAPTER 20

"**D**ON'T YOU DARE attempt anything," the man said. He was young with sleek, black hair combed to the side. He wore a faded button-up shirt and black pants with flip-flops that looked brand-new. He was handsome. "There is a firing squad outside the door, guns loaded and ready to fire. It's easy to replace you." The man had a deep and threatening voice that didn't match his kind-looking face.

Bé felt nauseated. She understood looks could be very deceiving. *He is not to be trusted. He's the enemy.* She wished she were Mèo's size, so she could hide behind the waste bucket in the corner too.

No one moved. Even Tuyết stayed silent. She had

her legs folded up against her body, her head tucked into her knees so that only her eyes showed.

The man turned and grabbed a rice pot from someone else on the other side of the door. He placed it in the center of the room next to the mostly empty water pitcher. He removed the pitcher, and the person on the outside handed him another one, as well as a stack of dishes, a large bottle of fish sauce, and a jar of dried, finely shredded pork that looked like lint. Then the door shut fully behind them.

"He will not have you," Cô Lan said after the man left. "Either of you girls."

Cô Bích served the food. There was only enough rice for each woman to receive two small bowls. They mixed the rice with shredded pork and fish sauce and chewed slowly, making each bite last. Bé ate only one and a half bowls. The other half she mixed with water for Mèo.

The kitten sniffed and ate some, but then left to go hunting. He swatted at small bugs and chased after invisible predators that the humans couldn't see.

Bé's stomach still ached in hunger, but two small bowls of rice was better than starving, and better than

Big Mother's spicy rice that burned her stomach. As she watched the women finish their meal, she thought of the days when she'd had plenty—when Má had still lived at home. She licked her lips remembering the braised fish, roasted chicken, stir-fried rice, soup, and fresh fruit they'd eaten for lunch and dinner. She thought about the coconut milk from the young coconut tree they'd grown. She thirsted for it. She even missed the ripe tamarind that she would eat from her tree.

The rice the men gave them was dry, and it hurt going down. The women ate in silence, and no one left even a grain of rice still sticking to the side of her bowl. Bé gulped down two cups of dirty water just to fill her belly.

The women watched Mèo in fascination as he stood on his back legs and used his remaining front paw to swat at the air. When he lost his balance, he fell and rolled over, exposing his stomach, as if he'd meant to do that all along. The woman closest to him rubbed his belly, and Mèo kicked at her hand with his three paws. She giggled, her eyes crinkling in delight.

The man returned an hour later. He removed the

dirtied plates, empty rice pot, and fish sauce bottle. Then, he and another man carried in two large tubs of water, soap, a stack of washcloths, and two empty metal bowls. They told the women to wash their bodies and their clothes, so they were fresh and clean for the selection.

*What is the selection?*

Bé looked at Ngân confused, and Ngân explained, "They pick four women to go with them every night."

"Up there, they let us bathe properly, dress us in fine clothes and perfume, feed us a full, proper meal. It's supposed to be an honor to be chosen," Cô Lan said with disgust.

"Only there's no way to leave. There is a guard with a machine gun outside the room," said a woman with a hoarse voice. "They remind you that you could die at any moment."

"Some don't come back," Ngân said.

*The work they do is dangerous*, Bé thought. She hoped she wasn't chosen. What if she made a mistake, and a bomb she was working on blew? Would the women down here also explode?

"I wager we don't get a proper funeral either. Probably throw us in the ground somewhere and forget about us," said Cô Bích. "You stay here long enough, a quick death by bullet is a mercy."

"You're not thinking of—" Cô Lan's eyes widened.

"No," Cô Bích said. Then, after a long silence, she added, "Maybe."

The women began washing themselves and their clothes. All had bruises and scars—green and purple blemishes on their wrists and forearms, injuries on their chests and backs. Some of their wounds were healed completely, others were new. Several winced as they ran damp washcloths over their bodies. Bé wondered what could have caused all the injuries. *These men must be heartless masters. Maybe even worse than Big Mother.*

Bé touched her forehead scar and wondered how faded it had become, how long she'd be marked by Big Mother's cruelty. She yearned for a mirror to look, but there was nothing like that in the room, nothing but the water pitcher and the waste bucket. No furniture. Nothing to give the women comfort.

The women helped one another wash hard to reach

places, and they shampooed each other's hair. When it was Ngân and Bé's turn, they washed together, the older girl rinsing off the younger girl's neck and back. Bé didn't think using washcloths dipped in soapy water cleaned very well, but it left her feeling less sweaty and cooler. She pretended she was bathing at home in front of the water well, bringing up buckets of water and splashing her entire body with it. That water had been cool and refreshing and made her feel squeaky-clean.

Ngân washed Bé's hair. It had been a long time since she'd had her hair clean. She liked the feeling of Ngân's nails as they scratched against her itchy head. It reminded her of how Má used to wash her hair and massage her head. *Will I ever stop missing you?* She silently asked.

Other questions flooded her mind: *Am I going to be underground forever like these women? Will I ever escape? Where will I go if I do? Can I even go home now that Big Mother sold me? Is it even safe to go home? How long will Ba and Xuân search for me? Can Cha find a place for me?*

Bé once thought that Ba would find a good match for her when she turned eighteen, and she'd be married off to a nice man, but that future was gone. *What kind of future do I even have now?* All the questions sucked the energy from her body and made her feel helpless.

When the bathing was done, the women worked together to wash their clothes and bedding.

"We don't wash our clothes every day," Ngân explained. "We have only what is on our backs, and you have to wait a long time for clothes to dry since we're underground."

Bé watched the women who laundered their clothing wrap blankets around their naked bodies while they waited for everything to dry.

Bé didn't want to wash her clothes, so while the women were busy at their task, she found Mèo, who was playing in the corner with something metallic that made noise every time his paws moved it. Bé picked him up and nuzzled her face into the feline's fur. The kitten mewed and swatted at Bé's nose.

Hours passed in the dim light, but she and the women had Mèo to entertain and comfort them. A furry glimmer of light in the dark.

## CHAPTER 21

"Can you show me where you're from?" Ngân asked, showing Bé a rock she kept in her pocket for drawing on the mud. Cô Lan had found it for her when she was aboveground.

Bé softened the mud wall with water and began to draw. She drew her father's property, making a circle for the chicken enclosure, a fat pig shape for the pigsty, and a rectangle for the house. She drew a stick figure of a round woman and wrote "evil stepmother" next to it, and another stick figure of a man with a cane and wrote "Ba."

"You can write? Did you go to school?" Ngân asked.

Bé nodded, then she wrote, "Until nine."

"I used to, too, when my parents were alive," Ngân said. "What happened to your mother?"

Bé drew her tamarind tree with its limbs growing all over and curves for its bushy leaves. She etched two lines for the road, and far down the road, she drew a stick figure of her mother next to a bus with the words "left." On the road, close to the tamarind tree and the house, Bé drew a stick figure with two dots for eyes and a sad face and wrote "me."

"Oh, sweet child, your mother abandoned you?" Cô Lan asked, sitting down next to the girls.

"How sad," Ngân murmured.

"I am terribly sorry," Cô Lan said softly.

Bé shook her head. Her mother hadn't abandoned her. But she looked at what she had drawn on the mud. The words "left" and "me" stuck out to her.

*What did my mother do?* The past year filled Bé's thoughts. She handed Ngân back her rock and sat down.

*A mother loves and protects. She doesn't leave her children. Má must have known what Big Mother was capable of.* Bé touched her forehead scar, and she thought of the beatings she had endured over the last year. She thought of the days she starved, while the rest of the family ate meat. She thought of eating the dog food to survive. She thought of sleeping in the pigsty and having no place to go for comfort. *Má did this. Má left me . . . defenseless.*

And almost a year later, she hadn't returned.

Bé swallowed, fighting the sadness that begged to consume her. She stared at the walls that surrounded her, at the low ceiling, at the door with no handle.

*I'm stuck here. There will be no escape. There's a firing squad outside the door. The handsome man said so. The evil one.*

Bé crumbled inside, the impossibility of the situation overwhelming her.

Mèo jumped in her lap, purring, licking Bé's hand. Cô Lan and Ngân hugged her. She hadn't been hugged like this, possibly loved like this, since Xuân's hug, and Má before that, when Má was still with her.

That night, Cô Lan and Cô Bích moved the waste bucket away from its corner.

"Quickly now, girls," Cô Lan said. "Squat behind, stay in the shadows, and don't make a noise."

Bé grabbed Mèo and tucked him inside the pocket of her shirt. She and Ngân did as Cô Lan had instructed. The women filled in around them, forming two tight lines, concealing the two girls and the makeshift toilet. She couldn't see anything from where she hid. Bé pinched her nose, though she could still smell the strong stench from the bucket.

The door creaked open. Bé heard a sharp inhale as the women held their breaths. The silence in the room was loud and terrifying, but the women stood tall, like a shield protecting the two young girls.

Bé heard footsteps enter the room. An old man's voice. "So many beautiful choices, and our clients are especially hungry tonight."

*Hungry?*

The woman standing closest to Bé flinched slightly. She and all the other women had hands balled up in fists. Some were shaking. Bé heard Tuyết crying softly, whimpering.

An uncomfortable silence passed. It felt like an

eternity. Bé looked at Ngân, who was as green as a raw tamarind. Mèo stirred, and Bé slid a hand into her pocket to silence his movements. She placed her finger in the cat's mouth. His tiny teeth nibbled down, and Bé hoped this would keep her kitten from making noise.

"Where is the new girl?" the old man asked. "I hear she is especially young. And pretty, too."

*Don't make a sound. Don't breathe.*

She heard shuffling. Someone fell and yelped.

"Where is she?" The old man's voice. "Get out of my way."

Bé squeezed her eyes shut and tried to imagine she was anywhere but there. She focused on her happiest memories, when she was once loved. She remembered splashing in the neighborhood stream by her old house, of flying a kite with Ba, of catching snails in the paddy fields with Xuân, of climbing her tamarind tree, going higher and higher. She remembered her favorite lantern from the Mid-Autumn Festival when she was much younger. It was shaped like a fish with big eyes and a blue fin. She concentrated, remembering. Remembering.

She ignored the sounds of a scuffle, a gentle voice speaking in the background. The familiar voice was muted in Bé's ears like there was an ocean between her and them. Bé loved being near the ocean, the waves splashing, tickling her legs, the sand sticking to the bottom of her feet, chasing the crabs as they popped in and out of their holes along the shore. Bé tried to block out any movement, but a hand nudged her back.

She didn't want to open her eyes, but she heard Ngân's voice calling her. "Friend."

Ngân was calling her "friend." *She thinks of me as a friend.* She hadn't had a true friend in years, since she'd left Sang behind—only Xuân, but he was her brother.

Bé opened her eyes. Ngân was peeking behind the waste bucket. Bé did the same. A space had opened in the shield of women. The old man was walking away, followed by Cô Lan, Tuyết, and two other women whose names Bé didn't know.

*No.*

There was a collective exhale from the women left behind as the door slammed closed.

"Cô Lan took your place!" Ngân said, standing up.

"Everyone fought to prevent them from finding us, and Cô Lan volunteered to go."

Mèo made an annoyed grunt and Bé let him loose. Her stomach churned, and she wanted to throw up.

"She'll be fine," Cô Bích said, her normally angry voice softening. "She's been selected many, many times."

Bé threw up in the waste bucket.

## CHAPTER 22

Bé couldn't sleep. Cô Lan had taken her place. She had saved her. She had protected her. Guilt gnawed at Bé. It was like what had happened to Xuân all over again, and she was to blame.

*"Your fault! All your fault!"* Big Mother's voice echoed in her memories.

Though she barely knew these women, they had protected her, shaded her from view like her tamarind tree.

Bé wasn't sure what happened to the women above, or what work they had to do. The women wouldn't speak about it. Bé thought that Ngân probably knew, because she was just as terrified of being selected. But Bé didn't want to ask. She didn't want to know. She didn't want to be more afraid than she already was.

Bé clutched the hem of her shirt where the broken rosary lay, and she prayed that Cô Lan would come back. *But what if she doesn't? What if she's like Má—gone forever? What if she's like Xuân and stops speaking to me?*

The hours passed slowly, like sap dripping from a rubber tree. Bé tossed and turned. It was murky black in the room, like poison, like death, like hopelessness. No one slept restfully, except for Mèo. He lay curled up on Bé's chest, his breathing rhythmic and lulling. Cats were lucky. Bé wished she were a cat.

Some of the women muttered in their sleep. Others screamed horrendous sounds.

At some point in the night, Bé fell asleep. When she awoke, Mèo was gone and Cô Lan lay on the floor next to her, cuddled in a tight ball, her face toward the wall. Her braid was a mess, bits of hair sticking out everywhere. A deep red, blotchy bruise was starting to form on her neck, the indentations of fingers pressed hard against her skin. Bé moved her hand to caress Cô Lan's hair, but she trembled at her touch.

"Don't," Cô Bích said. "She'll be better tomorrow."

"Unless they pick her again," said Út, one of the night screamers.

Ngân whispered, "They haven't picked anyone twice in a row yet."

Cô Lan lay in her ball, trembling on and off until the meal was served. When Mèo returned from his hunting in the shadows, he lay with her, snuggled into the crevice of her neck, purring. He licked Cô Lan's tears when they fell and head-butted her when she stirred. He chirped, trying to talk to her, but she didn't answer back. Cô Lan rubbed the top of his head occasionally, which made him snuggle in closer to her.

The same man came to bring the food. He didn't look at Ngân or Bé, but he inspected all the other women in the room. His hungry eyes flicked over each woman up and down, examining them like roasted duck hanging at the street market. Cô Bích scowled; the muscles in her jaw bulged, clenched. Tuyết moaned, looking away, clawing at her skin. Cô Lan stared at the man with black, vacant eyes.

Even after the man left, Cô Lan's face was blank,

expressionless. She looked past the women in front of her and gazed at nothing, unblinking for long seconds. Bé wondered where she was and if she would ever come back.

Mèo stayed on Cô Lan's lap, not budging once. Sometimes Cô Lan absently petted him. Bé hoped Mèo was helping Cô Lan feel better. Bé wished she could do something more.

Cô Bích dished out the rice and dried pork. The women ate, their voices a cacophony of anger and disgust.

"Last night can never happen again," said a woman Bé didn't know well. "They were too rough on them. They almost snapped Lan's neck. Look at her."

Cô Lan kept silent.

"I need a knife. Cut them where it hurts," Cô Bích said, voice hard and seething.

"You wouldn't survive!" Út said.

"I'm not a dog," Cô Bích said.

Ngân gave Bé a worried look. Cô Bích was angry, too angry.

"Don't do anything dumb," Út said.

Cô Bích said nothing the rest of the day. She

simmered, and Bé wondered what would happen when she boiled over.

Mèo rubbed his body against Bé's side. He meowed, quietly at first and then more loudly. Bé took a bit of rice, chewed it up, and fed it to him. Ngân gave him another bite. Even Cô Bích gave him a piece of her food.

Cô Lan placed down her half-eaten bowl. She flicked a handful on the ground for Mèo, and then divided the rest between Ngân and Bé before retreating to her corner to lie down.

The other women taken last night didn't say much. Dark bruises decorated their skin as well—on necks, arms, and faces. When they moved, they winced, like each step hurt.

Bé decided she wouldn't allow anyone else to take her place. The guilt was too much for her. Má had once said she was fierce like a tiger. She would be courageous when it was her time.

Cô Lan spent the rest of the day sleeping. Bé and Ngân sat beside her, playing with Mèo. The kitten jumped over the women's feet, up and down the wall, his little paws zooming around fast.

"How did he lose his paw anyway?" Ngân asked.

Bé drew on the mud wall and explained. Bé liked having this new way of talking without words. It made her feel a little stronger, a little less fractured.

She told Ngân the story of how she got her forehead tattoo, and how Big Mother forced Xuân to help.

Ngân sat in stunned silence, mouth open, eyes widening. When she finally spoke, she said, "What an evil woman." She shook her head. "She was jealous of you. You were your father's love child."

Bé considered this, then shrugged. She would never have sympathy for Big Mother.

The two girls spent the rest of the afternoon talking, Ngân with words from her mouth and Bé with drawing pictures and words on the wall. She told her new friend about Xuân and all the ways he'd helped hide Mèo. She told her about how her brother had liked to race her when they were young. She told Ngân about outrunning the man, but then how her stepmother had betrayed her.

"You must miss your brother," Ngân said, and Bé nodded. She hoped he was out there looking for her.

When they ran out of things to talk about, Ngân

taught Bé games and rhymes that they played with their hands. They played until their hands hurt. They both smiled, stealing a moment of joy in this dark place.

# CHAPTER 23

THE WOMEN shifted their positions in the line. Those who had been in the second row the night before moved up, and those in the first row stood behind. Cô Lan stood in the last row, her back curved and eyes glazed. Bé and Ngân hid in the shadows behind the waste bucket. Bé had wanted to stand with the women, to show she was not afraid of the men, but Ngân had pulled her behind the bucket and said, "Don't be stupid. It's too dangerous for us up there. We would not come back alive. This is our only way to survive." Bé had shuddered at her friend's words and stayed hidden.

"Changing places will not stop you from being chosen. You will all have your turn. It is an honor to be selected," said the old man. His voice was slow and gentle, but there was an increasing edge to his voice. He reminded Bé of how a snake would speak. "Yesterday's actions cannot be repeated, or you can choose which of your friends goes to the firing squad."

"We are getting fed up with your behavior!" shouted a deeper voice, younger. Bé recognized the voice. It was the man who brought their meals.

"You're fed up?" Cô Bích yelled indignantly.

Gasps rustled like a wave among the women.

"No! Don't!" Út's voice.

Cô Bích didn't stop. "You kidnap and cage us, and expect us to be thankful? NO! NO MORE! We will fight, and we will fight you until our last breath!" she snarled.

Bé and Ngân locked eyes, terrified.

The younger man shouted a string of profanities—words that would put Big Mother to shame. Then Bé heard heavy steps, like boots stomping into battle.

Bé closed her eyes and covered her ears. Her breath came hard. Her heart pounded.

The door opened and slammed loudly behind them.

There was a chorus of cries, and someone begged, "Please don't hurt her!"

A collective silence took over the room. Cô Bích had been taken.

Many long minutes later, the old man returned and cleared his voice. "Now, who will honor us tonight?" he said as if nothing had happened.

They proceeded to pick another four women—not Cô Lan, not Ngân, and not Bé. When the door shut, the women huddled around one another. A somber stillness filled the air.

"She won't be back. They will not let her live," rasped Út.

Ngân sobbed on Bé's shoulder, and Bé held her like she had held Bé the first night. Bé was too shocked to cry, to feel, to know what to think. She barely knew Cô Bích, but she knew that Cô Bích didn't deserve what happened.

Bé thought of Big Mother. At home, no one had protected her, but here, women had sacrificed themselves for her.

The night came and went. Cô Bích did not come back.

When morning light returned to the room, Cô Lan and the other women huddled around the place where Cô Bích had slept. Some women cried. Others prayed.

"May you be free from sorrow," they said to the empty space as if Cô Bích were there.

"May you fly away and be reborn into a land of peace and tranquility," Cô Lan said.

"O Lord, have mercy on her soul," prayed Út. "Be at peace."

Ngân only cried—she hadn't stopped crying since the night before. Bé held her and rubbed her back the way Má had when she was upset.

Mèo tried to comfort Ngân too. He sat on her lap and licked her bare arm as if he were giving her a bath. He rubbed his cheek against her and purred. Ngân sniffed and then picked him up and cried into his fur.

Bé's eyes were dry. She didn't know Cô Bích as well as everyone else. *Why did she fight back? Didn't she know it's safer to be silent?* Bé looked around the room at the suffering of the women. *Cô Bích was angry*, Bé thought, *and she was strong and brave. I hope I can be courageous like her.* Then she thought of Má. *Was she courageous? Did someone hurt her like they hurt Cô Bích? Is she even alive?*

Bé wondered where they would bury her, *if* they buried her. Bé remembered Cô Bích's words and shivered. *"I wager we don't get a proper funeral . . . probably throw us in the ground somewhere and forget about us."*

Bé resolved to never forget Cô Bích. The women in the room would remember her too. Her life would not be forgotten.

The women survived the next week in mourning. Ngân and Bé didn't play. They just held each other if one of them cried. Cô Lan looked even more distant, worry lines around her lips. The days seemed long and endless, and the nights scary and lonely.

The room felt smaller, emptier without Cô Bích. Like they were chickens in a cage with no place to run, waiting for the farmer to choose which one to eat for supper. Cô Bích had been the anchor that held the boat in place. Without her, the boat was sinking, splintered apart. The room was too quiet and somber. Even Tuyết barely muttered a sound.

No one had much of an appetite. They mostly picked at the rice. Everyone was silent during the meal, and quiet when they washed their bodies.

Mèo also lost his kitten energy. He spent his days sleeping on different women's laps and head butting them for pats when he was awake. At night, he chased shadowy, invisible predators. Once, he killed and ate a mouse.

When the old man came, the women formed tighter lines, hands linked together. Each night, Ngân and Bé escaped being chosen. Bé knew it was only a matter of time, though. There was a reason they had been sold; there was a reason the men had them.

"I overheard they are moving us to Thailand soon," Út said one morning. "Last night, I heard one of them say they're saving the young girls for Thailand. They'll fetch a higher price."

Bé's stomach twisted. Would she be separated from her new family of women? She didn't want to be. No one had cared for her as they had. She clutched Mèo close to her.

## CHAPTER 24

ONE NIGHT, two weeks after Cô Bích was taken, men with big guns barged in, shouting and awakening the women. "Up! Up! Or we will shoot. Get up now or die! You're moving!"

Strong hands grabbed Bé and hoisted her up. The cold, hard point of a gun's muzzle touched her cheek. Bé went numb. Her gut clenched and time slowed as fear gripped her body.

A man screamed, "Move! Move! Now!"

Bé's heart pounded, pounded, pounded. She did as the man commanded, moving on shaky legs. She stumbled. She was shaking so hard.

*Where's Mèo?*

It was dark, and her sleepy eyes hadn't adjusted. She

pretended to fall, dropping to her knees, hurriedly trying to feel the ground. She couldn't leave Mèo there.

Bé's head was yanked back. A man pulled her up by her hair and delivered a boot to her side, pushing her to the door. The sharp pain knocked her over. The air left her chest and refused to return.

"Move, stupid girl!"

All around her was chaos. Bé heard the scuffling and scrambling of the other women. Their cries. Their screams. No one seemed to be moving fast enough for the men with the guns.

"Faster! Hurry!" the men yelled.

The guns clicked. A man picked Bé up by the arm and threw her forward. She stumbled but managed to stay on her feet and scrambled toward the door. Bé passed through another room, similar to the one they'd been held in. They turned a corner and climbed stairs. Bé's calves burned from the effort. She staggered several times, and the man behind her cursed.

*Crack! Crack! Crack!*

Bé heard the faint sound of gunshots just as a gun's muzzle pressed hard against her back. Her feet moved, but fear pulled her down, down, down.

The threat of tears burned Bé's eyes. She was leaving Mèo behind, and she felt paralyzed from the inside out. How could she survive in this scary world without her beloved kitten? Mèo was all she had left of her old life. Mèo, whom she'd saved. Mèo, who had reunited her with Xuân. Mèo, who had stayed with her and comforted her in the dark.

Bé's chest tightened, and she slowed.

"Get a move on it! Now!"

*Mèo. My poor Mèo. Where is he? Did he get trampled? How will he find his way out of that maze?*

They climbed up six sets of stairs. Bé was panting and coughing when they reached the top. There was a lavishly decorated bedroom, paintings adorning the walls in a clash of yellow. Bé hesitated and turned, but the man behind her yelled. "Move!"

The men hustled them outside, where a truck was waiting. Some were already on it, huddled tightly together in two rows. Two armed men, holding massive rifles, stood on alert near the truck's cabin.

There was smoke in the air, and the smell of burning buildings invaded Bé's nostrils.

Bé's eyes and ears stung. Her whole body was screaming in pain. All she could think of was moving forward, farther away from the men with guns.

*Mèo*, she thought again. The thought of Mèo burning was like a punch in the gut. Bé could hardly breathe through the pain.

A bomb exploded in the distance. Bé turned to the sound. An orange glow had lit up the night. They were close to the fighting. Too close.

"Stop staring! Get a move on! Unless you want to burn with the rest of this village!"

Someone yanked Bé up and put her on the truck.

"Thank God!" gasped Cô Lan. Bé threw her arms around her and buried her face in the woman's chest. The woman stroked Bé's hair. Tears of relief fell from Bé's face. Cô Lan had survived. The woman who had taken care of her all those long nights was alive.

Bé waited anxiously as the men with guns forced woman after woman onto the truck. Finally, Ngân was hoisted up. She had her arms folded tightly across her chest and squeezed into a spot next to Bé.

Cô Lan motioned for Bé to move toward the end

of the truck. Another armed man hopped on, just as the truck began moving down the road. Bé recognized him—he was the man who brought them their meals. He sneered, baring teeth and patting his rifle. Bé wished she could push him off the truck.

As the truck plodded along the road, the world behind them lit up. Tiny figures with tanks strapped to their backs aimed a hose, emitting plumes of orange fire, burning everything in sight—thatched houses, trees and plants, animals. Even tinier figures ran out of homes. A giant plume of black smoke spread and covered the village.

Everything behind them was on fire.

*Méo. My sweet Mèo.* Gone like everyone else she'd loved. Má. Bà Nội. Xuân. Ba.

There were gunshots. A rhythmic cadence of *boom, boom, boom.* The farther they were from the village, the fainter the sounds became.

*How many people will escape? How many will die?*

The heady and ominous shadow of death hovered over the night, enveloping everything in its cloak, swallowing the world whole.

The war had never been so close, so real. Cô Lan pulled Bé tight to her chest.

Bé wanted to go home, where the fighting was far away, and she could pretend the war wasn't real. But now she couldn't run. She couldn't pretend this wasn't happening. Death was real.

"Don't look," Cô Lan whispered. "War is not for young girls."

Bé glanced at Ngân, who had a mischievous glint in her eye.

"I have Mèo," Ngân whispered as the truck bumped along. She unfolded her arms and something from inside her shirt poked out.

"NO TALKING!" barked an armed man.

*Mèo!* Bé could hardly believe it. She wanted to cry. She wanted to jump up and down in joy. But the men kept a close eye. Relief spread across her face—she was so relieved that her cat hadn't died.

The gray striped kitten shook, his fur all rumpled and ragged. When the guards weren't looking, Ngan handed Mèo to Bé. He clambered on Bé's lap, purring. Bé slipped him inside her chest pocket. He was growing big, and the pocket was snug. He didn't wiggle or try to escape. But Bé worried. *How will I keep Mèo with me?* She squeezed him close, filling her view with Méo's fluffy face and button nose. He licked her with his sandpaper tongue.

Cô Lan's eyes surveyed the truck, the armed men, and the grate that kept them from falling off. She whispered something to Út, who was sitting next to her. Bé couldn't hear what she said, but Út nodded and whispered to the woman next to her.

Ngân laced her fingers in Bé's.

The truck jostled along. The ride was bumpy and uncomfortable, but Bé breathed in the night air—crisp and fresh, not like the stale air she had been inhaling for the past two weeks. They were far enough away from the burning village now that there was only a hint of smoke that still lingered in the air, like the scent of a burning candle after it's been blown out.

Bé gazed up at the night sky, trying to tune out the sounds of gunfire and explosions in the distance. She remembered Má's voice telling her the story of Chú Cuội. Bé let herself become lost in the stars. The moon was full and bright, just like the last night with Má.

*"I will miss you and I'll always look for a way back to you. I promise,"* Má's voice whispered in her memories. How she wished Má was there. How she wished she could be up on the moon with Chú Cuội. She stared up at the moon until her eyelids went heavy and sleep took her.

## CHAPTER 25

Bé DREAMED of her tamarind tree, the soft rustle of its fruit-laden branches in the summertime breeze. Its soothing melody calmed her even on the worst day. It was a lazy summer afternoon, when she was nine. Xuân cracked the hard, outer shell of a tamarind fruit for her, and she tasted the sweet, sticky goodness of the fruit inside. The first ripe fruit of the season always tasted the best. Then Xuân was teaching her to climb the tree. She was scared at first, but with her brother at her side, she became fearless, climbing higher than he ever dared.

A high-pitched whistle shrieked in the distance, followed by an ear-shattering BOOM.

Bé jolted awake. She blinked the sleep from her eyes

and pulled herself upright so she could see over the back of the truck. The sun was just peeking through the mountains on the horizon, but plumes of orange flashes and gray smoke shadowed everything behind them. Tiny figures, like little fire ants escaping their mound, ran from the blasts, hands outstretched, feet stumbling. Some caught each other; others fell. Smoke covered them all. Bé's eyes pricked with tears, and she wanted to scream, *Run! Run faster!* She wished she could save them all. The tiny shapes became minuscule and disappeared from sight as the truck jostled along the bumpy road.

The truck dodged and swerved through blasts, mortars, and bombs. The women, packed together as tight as sticky rice wrapped in banana leaves, moved as one, leaning left and right, jerking forward and backward as the truck moved along. Bé felt motion sick. This was the first time she'd ever been in a vehicle like this. It was disorienting and made her stomach lurch upward. She grabbed onto Ngân's hand. Her friend looked green, too.

There were bicycles and motorbikes all around them, everyone trying to outrun the war. *No one can escape*, Bé thought.

The truck lurched and swerved suddenly, knocking everyone sideways.

"MORTARS!" someone yelled. "FASTER! DRIVE FASTER!"

Explosion after deafening explosion, each one closer and closer, slammed against the truck. Bé couldn't help it. She vomited. It was mostly water and bile, and it went everywhere, spilling over her lap and trickling down her legs. Cô Lan rubbed her back and Ngân held back her hair as she retched. When her stomach was empty, she leaned against Cô Lan, feeling miserable.

After several long minutes, Ngân squeezed her hand and said, "When we grow up, I want to live on a boat and become a fisherwoman. You and me together. Floating down the Mê Kông River, catching freshwater crabs and shrimp and fish. Safe and free and away from bad men and bombs."

"Hold on to that dream," Cô Lan said.

Bé shut her eyes, thinking about the last time she'd tasted crab. She ignored the sounds of explosions and the jostles of the truck and concentrated on a memory of long ago. She pretended the explosions were the firecrackers during Tết. She remembered Má and Ba taking her to the night market during the lunar new year holiday when she was little. Ba carried her in his arms, so she wouldn't get lost among the throngs of people. They squatted on the ground in front of an old wooden table, watching a skinny lady chargrill crab over an open fire bursting with flames, using chopsticks to flip the crab when it was burned on one side. She remembered the fragrant smell of the cooked crabmeat and how she licked all her fingers clean.

Bé opened her eyes and stared at the man sitting at the end of the truck with his rifle. *When I am grown, I want to live by the ocean in a little house with my cats. I'll fly kites with Xuân and Ngân, who will live nearby, and I'll be free to do anything I choose.*

She held the image in her mind, imagining the feeling of the ocean breeze on her face, the smell of salt and sea in her nostrils, the weight of the kite in her hands. It was an impossible dream, but it was hers.

A volley of mortars rained down nearby.

There was chaos on the truck. Women were screaming at the armed men, begging to leave the truck, to take their chances with the war. The women looked bold with their loud mouths, but their shoulders were trembling. Bé was trembling too.

Bé and Ngân cuddled in closer to Cô Lan. Cô Lan put her arms around them and said, "You girls are strong. And now, you must be very brave. This is your chance. When I tell you, I want you to run as fast as you can. Don't look back, and don't worry about me. I'll be fine."

Before Ngân or Bé could react, Cô Lan unwrapped them from her embrace and stood. A second later, she lunged at a sneering guard.

"No! Cô Lan!" Ngân screamed, but her voice could barely be heard over the chaos on the truck.

Cô Lan kicked the guard hard in the groin. She screamed, "Now!"

A gun went off—maybe from the guard Cô Lan kicked or someone else. Bé couldn't tell because a mass of women's bodies had swarmed the armed guards.

Arms and legs surrounded Bé, many women tangled with only a few men who were like fish caught in a net, and before Bé knew what was happening, someone was hoisting her over the back of the truck and screaming at her.

"Run! Don't die here! Run! Run! Run!" Cô Lan's voice.

Bé's mind swirled. Where was Ngân?

"RUN!"

Bé ran. Mèo stirred in her pocket. She held her hands over him and ran as fast as she could, legs pumping, tears wetting her lashes, moving toward the paddy fields. She could hide there. They were lower than the road.

In her ear, she heard Xuân's voice saying, "Pretend the Việt Cộng are coming. Run to that fork ahead! How fast can you run? Can you catch me?"

But it was no longer pretend danger. The Việt Cộng were there. She was escaping the war. She pumped her legs even faster. They felt weak and unsteady after weeks of being underground, but she pretended her brother was ahead and she was going to beat him this time. She would win their race. She had no choice. She had to survive.

Motorbikes and bicycles whizzed past her. Her chest pounded like the gong ringing at home in the local

Buddhist monastery. Her legs twinged and spasmed, but instinct forced her to keep moving, her feet landing hard with each pump. She ran through the pain in her chest, through everything.

Mèo chirped a small meow in her chest pocket, giving her comfort as smoke surrounded her, snaking its way into her lungs, choking her. She coughed and stumbled. She couldn't see in front of her, and she could barely make out the ground beneath her bare feet.

A small hand grabbed hers. "Friend!" A familiar voice.

*Ngân!*

"Stay together!"

With her free hand, Bé pressed her kitten closer to her, and the three ran together.

The smoke was clearing, and they were almost to the rice paddy fields. Bé's side cramped and she stumbled. Her legs were shaking so hard that they almost gave out, but Ngân was there, pulling her up. They stopped for a moment to catch their breath.

Bé tried to speak to her friend. She *wanted* to talk for the first time in a long time. But she coughed and nothing came out. So she did the only thing she could. She grabbed Ngân and hugged her tight. Mèo squeaked unhappily in between them.

*We're brave, just like Cô Lan said.*

When they parted, Ngân said, "We're finally free."

*BOOM!* An invisible fist punched Bé hard in the chest. Her ears filled with pressure, ringing so loudly that the world went silent. Then she was in the air, falling, falling. Time slowed, and for a second, she was like a bird. Flying. She folded her arms over her chest, protecting Mèo. The kitten's claws dug into Bé's shirt, sinking into her skin.

Fragments flew in the air above her, closer to Ngân, who was higher in the sky. Ngân tried to reach out to her, but a second later, Bé was tossed onto the cool marsh of the rice paddy fields and the world faded away.

# CHAPTER 26

"Mew!" Something wet and soft was pawing at Bé's face.

Bé slowly blinked her eyes open. The blue sky was blinding, so she squeezed her eyes shut again. It had been too many days in the dark, and her eyes were sensitive to the light. Daylight. It was day, and she was alive. She wasn't trapped anymore.

Bé tried to get up, but she couldn't move. She was broken. She ached in places she didn't realize she could ache. Her head throbbed. She was lying in a pool of liquid. It was wet and sticky in some parts.

She turned her head toward Mèo, and he nuzzled her nose. Thank goodness he was still with her. He had been safe cushioned in her chest pocket. She had protected him during her fall.

Just past Mèo, Bé saw green rice blades and muddy water.

The paddy fields. She was lying in the middle of the paddy.

Bé tried to wiggle her fingers, but everything hurt. She thought for a moment that she'd never be able to move again. Then a coughing fit forced her body upright. When she tried to move her left arm, a wave of excruciating pain hit her like a tidal wave during typhoon season. She looked down at her arm. It had snapped, the bones bent like a triangle underneath mud-stained skin. She screamed then—a soundless scream, then real, and high and unrestrained. Then it was gone.

People were rousing from the paddy fields; many looked bewildered, examining their body parts. Some shrieked for help, while others were stunned into silence. The road was strewn with rumpled bodies and busted bicycles and motorcycles.

Bé wondered about the truck. *Had the women escaped? Or were their bodies on the road?*

*Cô Lan . . . Út . . .*

Inside her heart, Bé knew she'd never see them again.

Bé began to shake. She was in so much pain. In her arm. In her heart. Everywhere. Everyone she loved had been taken away from her. Every single one. It wasn't fair.

"Friend."

*Ngân!*

Hope filled Bé. She looked around for the only friend she had left. Despite the raging pain that tore at her, she attempted to stand, but her legs were too shaky, and they gave underneath her, pulsing with a pain more horrible than Big Mother's worst beating. She heard Ngân's voice again.

"Friend." It was faint, like a whisper carried on the wind.

Mèo took off in the direction of Ngân's voice, hobbling on his three paws. He mewed as he went.

Determined, Bé crawled through the mud, following her cat over green rice stalks, biting down hard to squash the pain. When she finally reached Ngân, she nearly collapsed, white sparks in her vision.

Ngân's body was crumpled and muddy. She held her hands over her belly in pain.

Bé held her uninjured hand over Ngân's belly and realized her friend was bleeding.

Ngân whimpered, "The men are gone. They can't hurt us anymore."

Mèo licked Ngân's ear, and Bé dug deep into herself and screamed with the little energy she had left, waving wildly at everyone nearby. Her scream was a squeak, her voice retreating inside her. A middle-aged woman and a teenage boy ran toward them. Both had open gashes on their faces.

The woman ordered the boy to pick up Ngân and take her to the road. The woman tried to help Bé up but they both sank back into the mud.

"The southern army is here. They will help," the woman said to Bé. She made a motion, but Bé's eyes fluttered closed.

She heard Ngân's weak voice whisper, "Sir, our cat. Don't leave our cat."

Bé heard Mèo mew twice before she felt steady hands picking her up like she was a rag doll and placing her on a flat surface. An engine roared to life underneath her. *I'm in another truck*, Bé thought. But this time, they were taking her to safety.

The voices of men and women surrounded her. They used words she didn't understand. A needle poked into her arm. She heard a soft mew. Sandpaper tongue on her bare feet.

A woman's voice said, "Cat, get off her."

*Mèo*, Bé thought as the world disappeared into stripes of gray.

# PART 4
## SHE IS MY SISTER

## CHAPTER 27

Bé WAS SOARING high above the paddy fields, floating away from muddy squares full of injured people, then across land to the decimated village where she had been kept prisoner. As she flew, she drifted farther back in time.

She was five years old, running between Ba's legs. Má swooped her up and spun her around. She giggled. Then she was racing down the lane toward the neighbor's house to see their new piglets, Xuân running next to her. Suddenly, Great-Uncle Five's monkey appeared and yanked her hair, but Xuân was there to save her. As Xuân and the monkey disappeared, Cô Lan and Ngân were there, standing on a boat. The other women from the underground bunker, too. They waved from the boat while she stood at a river's edge. Then she saw Má on the boat blowing her kisses. The boat began to push off from the riverbank, but Bé couldn't move. She was stranded, frozen on the land. Ngân stepped off to grab her hand, but she couldn't reach. Bé screamed as the boat floated down the river, carrying all the women she loved away from her.

Bé's eyes fluttered open. A masked man gazed down at her. He said something—she couldn't catch the words—but she noticed his gloved hands, his eyes widening, his frantic wave. She felt a sharp sting of a needle, and then warmth spread throughout her. The dark took her again. She heard the crack of a bone, but she felt no pain.

For how long she was floating in the dark, she didn't know. She didn't care.

Then someone was stroking her cheek. It was the strangest sensation. Like a tickle, only she didn't want to giggle. Her mind told her to wake up, but her eyelids were heavy, her body tingly and numb. She couldn't move, and she didn't want to. She wanted to sleep, needed to find a way to get back on that boat with Má,

Ngân, and Cô Lan. She kept her eyes closed, hoping to drift off again.

"Drink. Just one sip," a woman's voice said, soothing as a canary's song. Bé used to love canaries and the songs they sang.

Bé felt a drip of water on her mouth, and she parted her lips. She drank, eyes closed. Someone else was holding the cup, because she couldn't feel her fingers. She didn't realize how parched she was until she swallowed and the water soothed the fire burning in her throat. It was clean water, not metallic, not dirty. It felt like it had been years since she had tasted water this good.

"Slow now. I have plenty," the woman said.

Bé still didn't open her eyes as she drank. When she was finished, she sighed soundlessly.

*Mèo. Where is he? Was he left at that paddy field? Was he still in the truck . . . ?*

Bé fell back asleep.

Bé dreamed Mèo was roaming that paddy field, happy and free, chasing mice and birds and lazing in the sun. Bé remembered the soothing vibrations of his purrs and how soft his fur felt against her skin.

It was night when Bé woke again. She opened her eyes for a minute, but then closed them again. It was dark, and she was tired. She didn't know how much time had passed or how long she had been in the bed. Her clothes were soaked through with sweat. It was hot in the room, though she could hear the whirring of the overhead fan and the sounds of others shifting in beds, some moaning, others snoring loudly.

Bé opened her eyes again. There was a woman sitting next to her bed.

*She's beautiful*, Bé thought, like how she imagined an angel to look.

The woman smiled. Her heart-shaped face was tanned and smooth with only a spattering of freckles on her cheeks. Her hair was neatly pinned up in a bun, and she wore a light blue áo dài. She was probably older than Má by a decade, but her smile reminded her of Cô Lan's. The thought of Cô Lan made Bé's chest tighten. She prayed for the impossible that Cô Lan was all right.

"Are you hungry?" the woman asked.

Bé slowly nodded and the effort exhausted her. She closed her eyes and heard shuffling. Footsteps retreating. Minutes passed, and then the woman was back. "Tomorrow, I will bring you good food. Tonight, you eat cháo."

The watery rice porridge was tasteless, but it was easy to swallow and filled her empty stomach. Cháo was always her least favorite food; something Má only fed her when she was sick. She guessed she must be very sick now.

With her belly full, Bé fell back to sleep.

As the days passed, Bé would wake a few times during the day, but never for too long. Each time, she would find that the nice woman was never far from her bed. She'd feed her cháo and make sure Bé had enough water to drink.

Once, Bé thought she heard a familiar meowing coming from an open window in the hospital room. She struggled to look, but her eyelids hung too heavy and sleep soon found her.

Slowly, Bé regained feeling in her arms and legs, though her right arm and left leg were each in a hard cast. Her head was also bandaged.

When Bé slept, she dreamed of home, of Bà Nội

cutting up slices of watermelon for her and Xuân, of Má brushing her hair and dressing her up to take her to the Tết market, of riding the buffalo with Xuân and Ba. She dreamed of her life when she had been the happiest.

## CHAPTER 28

AFTER MANY WEEKS, Bé woke to find the woman wasn't there. Daylight filtered through the windows. The electric fan overhead hiccupped, clicked, then swirled the humid air around her. Bé gazed at it, then at the yellow walls, and then down to her broken arm and leg. The fingers and toes in her broken limbs felt tingly and numb. She tried to lift them, but the pain made her wince.

*Ngân.* It was the first time she'd thought of her friend in days. Guilt tore at her. She gathered all her strength and propped herself up onto her good elbow and looked around.

The room was overcrowded with beds, each of them occupied, but Ngân wasn't here. Bé's stomach clenched.

She needed to find out what happened to her friend. Ngân was all she had left.

The woman in the bed to Bé's left groaned in her sleep. The sound reminded her of poor, tongueless Tuyết. *Maybe it's better to die quickly*, Bé thought.

Bé looked away from the groaning woman. The old man to her right was pale, his translucent skin almost blue.

She lay back down and watched the fan whirl on the ceiling. The padded bed soothed her aching back. It had been almost a year since she'd slept in a bed like this.

"Ah, you're awake."

Bé watched as the woman who had been taking care of her approached, pushing a small cart.

"Are you hungry? The doctor said you can have real food now. I brought you some pork bánh bao today." She picked up the bamboo steamer basket from the cart beside her. She pulled out a warm pork bun and handed it to Bé.

Bé inhaled the food. She filled her empty stomach with pork, mushrooms, sausage, and eggs. Ba had given her a pork bun that day by her tamarind tree when she had gone two days without eating and had slept in the pigsty to hide. The food comforted her then, and it did so again. It felt like years had passed since that day in the tree. She missed Ba. She missed Xuân. She missed Ngân and all the women in the bunker. And she desperately missed Mèo.

Bé ached inside.

The woman sat next to Bé's bedside. "It's good to see you awake. After your surgery, I was worried you weren't going to make it. Your sister almost didn't."

Bé choked on her food. *Does she mean Ngân?* She looked at the woman, eyes wide, expectant.

"The nurse will tell you more, but don't worry, she's alive."

Bé let out a shuddering breath. *Alive. Ngân is still alive.*

"My name is Cô Huệ, by the way," the woman said. "I was here taking care of my sister-in-law when you were brought in. You had no one to care for you, and the nurses and doctors are short-staffed, so I stayed to help." She smiled, and Bé smiled back, thankful. "What's your name?"

Bé shook her head, pointed to her throat, and shook her head again.

A nurse and two orderlies entered the room. They covered the old man with a blanket and removed his body. He was dead.

Bé withdrew into herself. She couldn't escape death no matter where she went.

A nurse approached Bé's bed. She had a stern face, permanent frown lines around her eyes and mouth, and reminded Bé of an attack dog. Bé wanted to be left alone.

"I believe she's mute," Cô Huệ said.

The word made Bé shrink back even more. She wished she were a turtle and could slide into the safety of her shell and stay there. The word reminded her of Big Mother when she used to tell their neighbors, "She's a mute and very stupid." The neighbors would look at her pityingly and coo their sympathy to Big Mother. Bé hated everyone thinking she was stupid.

The nurse did not smile at Bé, and she spoke in a barking tone. "Wiggle your toes for me. Now your fingers. Good. The swelling's gone down. But you still have pain, hmmm?"

Bé nodded and did as she was commanded. The nurse tapped the back of the girl's hand. "Can you feel that?"

Bé shook her head.

"The nerves on your hand are damaged. The doctors aren't sure if the sensation will return. There's a good chance you'll never be the same." The nurse spewed the information with no feeling in her voice.

Bé stared at her hand. *Damaged forever. Like I am.* She felt fractured, as if she would never be whole again. Like the smashed rosary beads that Big Mother had stomped on.

"Oh, poor girl," Cô Huệ said. She tenderly caressed the top of Bé's head.

"We will keep you on pain medication, and then ease you off slowly," the nurse finished. She turned to one of the orderlies, who handed her a syringe. The nurse injected the medicine into Bé's arm. It stung but her pain melted away.

"There was a girl about your age who was brought in with you. She's your sister?" the nurse asked, and Bé nodded emphatically, jabbing a finger toward herself.

"Your sister was badly hurt in the mortar explosion. A fragment of the mortar bomb pierced her intestines. She's still alive, but it's not looking promising. We will bring her here to be with you if her condition stabilizes."

*Ngân, you can't die.* Bé had never felt so alone.

"... your parents ... village ... are you listening?" The nurse snapped a finger in front of Bé.

"You're scaring her," said Cô Huệ's voice.

"We need to locate your parents. Where are you from?" the nurse asked, more gently this time. "What is your name?"

*My parents, my name*, Bé thought. How could she explain everything that had happened to her? That she didn't know where Má was . . . that her stepmother had sold her . . . that the women who had helped her, who had become her family, might have died to save her.

*I have to try*, she decided.

Bé made a writing motion with her hand. The nurse pulled a pencil and pad from her pocket, and Bé scribbled down her father's name and the name of her village. Her handwriting was big and sloppy.

"You're over two hundred kilometers away from

home, on the other side of the country. We're near the Cambodian border," the nurse said.

"Oh, you've traveled quite a distance," Cô Huệ said.

Bé blinked.

Cambodia was a country that sat between Vietnam and Thailand. *Was this where the men were taking us? What about Thailand? Didn't Út hear that they were moving us to Thailand, where me and Ngân would be worth a higher amount?* Bé didn't want to think about the horrible men who had trapped her underground, the men with guns. She pushed the image from her mind.

*Ngân, you have to live.*

Bé clutched at the hem of her shirt . . . Wait, this was a white hospital gown. Where was her old shirt?

"We will send word to your parents," the nurse said.

Bé pointed wildly at her chest. Cô Huệ tilted her head, not understanding. Bé scribbled down that she wanted her shirt.

The nurse explained that Bé's shirt had fallen into tatters during the mortar attack and her ensuing transport to the hospital. They had thrown it away. It was gone.

Bé looked at the nurse in disbelief, jaw open.

Her shirt had been the only remnant that connected her to Má, who had bought it new; to Xuân, who had helped her save Mèo, her kitten who had slept and hidden in its pocket. Her rosary that Cha had given her. Everything that remained of her old life was gone.

## CHAPTER 29

Bé DIDN'T WANT to face the world. In the days that followed, Bé spent most of her time sleeping. She didn't dream. She felt like a discarded coconut husk. She let her missing consume her. She missed Xuân. She missed Má. She missed Ngân and Cô Lan. She missed her sweet Mèo.

Bé only woke when Cô Huệ nudged her to eat. Cô Huệ brought her delicious foods to try to lift her spirits—gỏi cuốn, spring rolls stuffed with shrimp, pork, and vegetables; bánh mì sandwiches filled with roasted chicken and sweet pickled vegetables on French bread; bánh chưng, sticky rice cake with mung beans and pork; coconut cassava cake; and sticky chè desserts. Eating helped, but it didn't heal the crack in her heart or bring anyone back.

During one of Cô Huệ's visits, Bé thought she saw a gray striped cat perched on the hospital room's windowsill. He looked at her and meowed, but then a nurse shooed him away and closed the window.

*It couldn't have been Mèo*, Bé thought. He was bigger than her cat. It was just her imagination.

Some days, Cô Huệ sat by Bé's bedside for hours, reading her books and telling her fairy stories of mythical creatures, dragons and fairies, magical swords, and ancient people who lived in Vietnam long ago. These stories reminded her of tranquil nights at home when Má had whispered the same tales as she'd drifted off to sleep. She'd never have moments like that again, and soon, Cô Huệ's stories would be gone. The idea left a bitter taste in her mouth.

*If Má hadn't left, I wouldn't be here. None of this would have happened.*

Bé's anger simmered. She was angry at Má. She was angry at the war. She was angry at the world.

Bé watched the hospital patients as they came and

went. Some stayed for only a day, others for longer. Some left with a sheet over their bodies. She eavesdropped on the nurses and doctors and learned her neighbors' stories. The boy to her left had lost his eye to a rubber band his cousin stretched and aimed at him. He didn't look much older than Bé. To her right, a skeletal woman lay with a broken back. She'd heard a rumor that the Việt Cộng were coming and had been so petrified that she'd scrambled underneath a table and broken her back.

Over time, Cô Huê's visits and meals did good work. Some of the other patients began to think that she was Bé's aunt, since she came to see Bé every day. And Bé began to look forward to the solace and comfort of her visits and her home cooking.

The nurses rarely had updates about her friend, but Cô Huệ told her that Ngân was still alive and recovering.

Bé woke up to a rhythmic purring and something heavy on her chest. She opened her eyes and found a ball of gray and white striped fur.

*Mèo!* Relief flooded her as she hugged him close with her good arm. *I thought you were lost for good. And you've grown!* She gave him a million kisses, and he purred in response. He licked away her tears with his sandpaper tongue.

It was dark in the room, the only light coming from the moonlight filtering through the window against the wall, its shutter having been left open. *Or propped open by a gray striped kitten*, Bé thought, smiling as tears escaped her eyes. *Mèo, you sneaky cat.*

Bé tried to stay up with him as long as she could, petting him and snuggling him, but then her eyes became too tired and she fell back to sleep with a smile on her face, her first in a long time.

Bé woke to a nurse's hysterical voice. "Out! Get off her, you fleabag!"

Mèo jumped off Bé and zoomed over to the windows, now filled with morning light. He glanced back at Bé once from the windowsill, and then he was gone.

Bé wanted to yell at the nurse for scaring off Mèo. She opened her mouth, but nothing came out. So instead, she just gave her an angry scowl.

"No cats allowed in the hospital," the nurse said.

Mèo came back that night, and every night after, leaving in the early morning hours. He slept on Bé's chest and gave her comfort as she waited for news of Ngân.

## CHAPTER 30

Two orderlies wheeled a young girl into the hospital room and placed her to Bé's left. Bé's eyes lit up when she recognized Ngân's face. Her friend was pale but alive.

"It's good to see a genuine smile from you," Cô Huệ said, coming into the room behind the orderlies.

Ngân's stomach was bandaged, her black hair tangled as always, but her face was clean and eyes were bright. *When her cheeks fill out, she will be very pretty,* Bé thought.

Bé wondered about her own reflection. What did she look like after months of imprisonment and weeks in the hospital? Did her face look different? Had her forehead scar faded? Would Xuân or Ba recognize her?

"They kept telling me that my sister was waiting to see me," Ngân said softly. "I am happy you are here."

Bé wanted to tell Ngân about Mèo, but every time she tried, only a wheeze came out.

Bé reached over and squeezed Ngân's hand. She didn't want to let go, but after a few minutes Ngân drifted off to sleep. Bé watched the rise and fall of her chest as she slept. Ngân looked relaxed in her slumber, and Bé hoped her dreams took her somewhere nice, away from the underground. Maybe Ngân had a "before," too, when her life was happy.

When Mèo came that night, Ngân was deep asleep, and when she woke the next morning, he'd already escaped out the window.

Bé wondered what Mèo did during the day. He was growing bigger and bigger. *Someone must be feeding him*, Bé thought.

Cô Huệ arrived shortly after she woke. She sat at Ngân's bedside and spoon-fed her cháo.

Afterward, the nurses came to change Ngân's bandages.

A week passed as Bé patiently waited for Ngân to gain her strength. Finally, Cô Huê arrived with cháo for both girls. Bé's rice porridge had fat pieces of poached chicken on top, while Ngân's was plain with sliced ginger. The cháo was warm and comforting in Bé's belly, and the chicken was full of delicious garlicky flavor.

After the girls finished their meal, Cô Huệ said, "With both of you much better now, I have so many questions. I'm dying to know what happened to you. Why are you so far from home? Has your sister always been mute? The scar on her forehead—what caused that? It wasn't from the explosion, was it?"

Ngân looked at Bé, and Bé made a writing motion with her uninjured hand.

"Can you get a notepad for my sister?" Ngân asked.

Cô Huệ brought Bé a notepad and pencil. Bé drew the same scene she had drawn on the mud wall, of the tamarind tree, her father's property, the bus that took her mother away. She wrote, "Má left me. Then I stopped talking." She showed the pad to Cô Huệ, who blinked in disbelief.

"You talked when your mother was around?" Cô Huệ asked. Bé nodded. "How long ago was this?"

Bé wrote, "One year."

"Your forehead scar?"

Bé wrote, "Stepmother." And then she wrote and drew pictures. Her hands shook, remembering, but she wanted Cô Huệ to know. Cô Huệ had cared for her, taken care of her when she had no one else, and Bé wanted this memory to stop haunting her. She drew the rosary that she had lost. Big Mother stabbing her with the quill pen, her brother holding her down. The broken pieces scattered around her.

Ngân looked at the drawing, frowned, held Bé's hand, and didn't let go. Cô Huệ shook her head after reading and mumbled, "Who would do that to a child? This just breaks my heart."

Then she rummaged through her pocket and laid something on Bé's lap. It was a beautiful rosary, crafted with white round stones and a wooden cross at the end. Bé could hardly believe it. She thought, *a prayer for the impossible.* She held it between her fingers and prayed that she and Ngân would stay together.

Cô Huệ said, "Keep it. It's easy for me to get another one. I live next to the big cathedral nearby."

Bé wrote, "Thank you."

She looped it around her neck and kept her hands clasped around it.

"Do you know what happened to our cat? I asked the boy who carried me from the rice paddy fields not to forget our cat, but then everything became fuzzy and I woke up here," Ngân asked.

Bé started to write in her notepad, "I know where—!"

"Is your cat a three-footed one with gray stripes?" Cô Huệ asked, and Bé looked up.

"Yes!" Ngân said. "And he likes chasing invisible things, and he's good at killing mice. Do you know where he is?"

"He's safe," Cô Huệ said, grinning.

Bé sat up straighter in the bed. *Cô Huệ knows Mèo?*

"The hospital doesn't allow animals, but I imagine he'll be waiting for you girls outside when you're released. He follows me back and forth from the hospital to my home every day. He's a smart little thing."

So Cô Huệ had been feeding Mèo, just as she'd fed and comforted Bé.

"I will tell you the rest of our story now," Ngân said. "And how we ended up here." She told Cô Huệ about the underground bunker, about the men and the selection. She didn't tell her that different people had sold her and Bé. She talked about the escape in the middle of the night, and how she didn't know if the women had survived or not. Ngân began to cry.

Cô Huệ wrapped her arms around Ngân. Then she waited a long moment before she spoke. "This should never have happened. After you're released, if you ever find yourself in trouble again, come find me here and I will help."

Bé and Ngân nodded.

"They are moving you to the orphanage in the next few days, while they wait for your father to reply. They need the beds at the hospital for the injured," Cô Huệ said.

"We can't go with you?" Ngân asked.

Bé didn't want to go to the orphanage. An orphanage meant she had no parents, nowhere she belonged, and she wanted to belong to Cô Huệ. She might have died in the hospital if Cô Huệ hadn't taken care of her. But Cô Huệ didn't want her, or else she wouldn't be sending her away.

Cô Huệ shook her head. "I wish you could come home with me, but they won't allow me to take you until they find your father. You'll be safe in the orphanage." Her face was stricken, and Bé knew that she was just as sad as she was.

At least she and Ngân would be together. No one would ever separate them again.

As Cô Huệ gathered her things to leave, Bé offered her back the notepad and pencil. Cô Huệ took them, but then placed them down next to Bé. "So you can find your voice again," Cô Huệ said.

Bé wrapped her arms around Cô Huệ and squeezed, wishing she could say, *Thank you, for everything.*

Ngân hugged her too and said, "We hope we will see you again one day."

Cô Huệ smiled and said, "Take good care of each other." Then she left them.

That afternoon, Bé used her notepad to tell Ngân about Mèo and his nighttime appearances.

"I want to see him!" Ngân said, but she fell asleep before Mèo came.

Bé nudged her awake, and when Ngân saw Mèo, she squealed loudly, waking up some of the other patients, who scowled at the girls.

Ngân squeezed him so hard that he hissed a little, then escaped to Bé's lap.

As Bé petted him, she worried about how to keep him with her at the orphanage. *What if I lose him again? He's too big to hide in any pocket now.* She scratched behind his ears and listened to him purr. *Maybe you'll be okay. You know where Cô Huệ lives, and maybe she'll help take care of you, too.* This thought gave Bé hope.

## CHAPTER 31

A FEW DAYS LATER, the girls were released from the hospital to the orphanage. Ngân was eating easily and full of energy, and the doctor removed Bé's casts. She could walk and use her arm, but she was still unsteady on her feet. As they walked outside to the hospital court-yard, she leaned on Ngân from time to time for support. It would take practice before she would walk normally again, the doctor told her, but children bounced back quickly.

Bé sat on a stone bench outside the hospital while Ngân ran around calling for Mèo as they waited for the hospital to make their travel arrangements. She placed two sets of clothes the hospital had given them next to her. The air was humid and sticky, and the sky looked like a storm was brewing. Their hair stuck to their sweaty faces, but they didn't mind. The girls loved being outside and breathing in the fresh air.

High concrete walls surrounded the hospital complex, protecting it from the outside. There was a gravel courtyard to their left and trees flanking each side of the walkway.

Bé took in the fresh air, the scents and smells, the sounds. Ngân seemed in good spirits as she made mewing sounds, running up and down the walkway, going up to different trees and looking into the branches.

Bé felt like an entire lifetime had passed since Big Mother had sold her to the man on the motorbike. So much had happened. Her stomach flip-flopped with nerves as she wondered what life would be like in the orphanage.

Bé looked down at the new beige, collarless, button-up shirt the hospital had given her to wear and crisp black pants. Her new notepad and pencil fit perfectly in her pants pocket. It felt strange being in new clothes. Ngân was wearing clothes that matched Bé's. *We look like we are truly sisters now*, Bé thought.

The leaves rustled softly in the trees, and Bé

listened to the slight chatter of birds above. The sounds reminded her of being in her tamarind tree. She thought of Xuân and wondered if he missed her as much as she missed him.

*Will Ba actually come?*

Bé listened to the bits of conversation of nurses and doctors as they passed her, the crunch of their feet as they walked on the gravel in between the buildings. The city outside the hospital was muted, but Bé could make out the noise of traffic, the beeps of motorbikes, and the gears of bicycles. She thought she heard a mew.

"Mèo?" Ngân squinted, looking up at a nearby tree.

Bé followed her gaze. A cat with familiar stripes of gray sat perched on a low-hanging branch. It tilted its head and let out a familiar *mew.*

"Mèo!" Ngân exclaimed, holding her arms up for him. Bé wanted to run over to the tree and join them, but her newly healed legs were still weak and wobbly.

The cat meowed again. He scuttled down the tree and leaped straight into the girl's arms. Ngân brought him over to Bé, who squeezed her three-footed cat. Bé knew from his nighttime visits that he had gotten bigger, but now in the daylight, Bé could see just how much fatter he'd become since their days underground. His bones didn't stick to his skin like they had before, and his stomach was beginning to protrude a little. Cô Huệ had been feeding him very well. The girls took turns petting and squeezing their beloved cat, who had brought them so much joy in the dark.

Before long, one of the orderlies came out of the hospital, followed by a young nun wearing a simple white habit. She had a kind-looking face and was holding some papers. *Release papers*, Bé guessed. The girls stood and huddled close together, hiding Mèo under the bundle of clothes the hospital had given them.

"Come on, girls. Mother Superior is waiting for us," the nun said, leading the way to the outside gate.

The orderly waved down a Citroen taxi, which pulled to the curb where the group was waiting. It was a large black car with four doors, a long hood with round headlights, and a square grill that gave it a grumpy-looking face and eyes. The taxi reminded Bé of the story Cô Lan had told them about her father's fancy car. Bé wondered what Cô Lan would say if she were with them. Her insides ached thinking of her.

The taxi driver opened his door and walked around to pull the passenger door open. Ngân helped an unsteady Bé in.

"To the orphanage on the other side of town, as quickly as possible, thank you," the nun said.

Bé scooted over in her seat and set Mèo hiding under the extra clothes in the corner by the door. Ngân sat next to her friend, and the nun sat in the front seat to give the taxi driver directions. Mèo peeked his head out from the bundle and made a small squeak. Ngân scratched under his chin to comfort him.

The driver started the loud engine and off they went. Bé was beginning to get used to the hum of engines and the rumble of vehicles.

The city was busy and bustling. As she looked out the open window, Bé had never seen the streets crowded with so many bicycles, pedicabs, mopeds, trucks, and buses. Nearby, she watched a group holding hands to cross the street, weaving in between the traffic. Bicycles easily avoided them while mopeds honked and swerved around them. This city moved much faster than her village. She didn't like it. She felt like she had been transported to another world, one where she didn't belong.

There were unfamiliar scents—gasoline, sewers, food aromas, chemicals. The city smelled very different from her village. Much more industrial. Like she was on a different planet. It scared Bé.

They passed a long row of three-storied houses, some connected to each other, others separated with alleys and side streets in between. On the ground floor level, a barbershop had its doors open. A man wearing a white drape sat smoking a cigarette while a barber cut his hair. Next door was a dress shop with rows and rows of colorful fabric. Next to that, there was a café where old men and soldiers sat around drinking coffee and tea—a café like the one where Má used to work.

They passed food stand after food stand where girls their age sold fresh-baked breads, fruit juice, and chè desserts. There was even a cinema, decorated with posters of handsome actors and actresses, kung-fu fighters, and American cowboys. Bé had never seen a real movie, and she wondered if she ever would.

The taxi passed a tall hill with many steps leading upward, where an impressive stone cathedral sat. It was marked with big round columns and a high tower that protruded up to the sky.

"That's near where Cô Huệ lives," Ngân said.

The driver turned a corner. They passed a street market where women sat selling produce. There were baskets full of freshly caught fish and crab; vegetables, mint, and other herbs; and all of Bé's favorite fruits—dragonfruit, mangoes, rambutans, durian. She licked her lips, remembering how each fruit tasted.

"Mangosteens!" Ngân exclaimed. "I haven't had one in ages. We used to steal them from my neighbor's yard. They'd stain my hands and all my clothes, and Grandfather would get so mad."

Behind the market were rows of peddlers with carts full of plastic toys and trinkets, sweet rice cooked in bamboo tubes, colorful lanterns for the Mid-Autumn Festival. *I wonder what lantern Xuân will choose this year,* Bé thought. *Will Ngân and I get to celebrate the festival together?*

Finally, the taxi stopped in front of a towering metal

gate. As the nun paid the fare, the girls stepped out. Ngân carried the extra clothes in her arms with Mèo hidden inside. She gave Bé a knowing smile. Bé gripped her notepad and pencil tightly and watched as the nun walked toward the orphanage entrance.

"Follow me," she called back to them as the driver drove away without another word.

A guard stood in front of the outside gate, yawning. A tall stone wall, the same height as the metal gate, surrounded the complex on both sides. The spikes at the top of the gate looked like they could pierce skin, like the tip of the bamboo reed quill pen Big Mother had used to tattoo Bé's forehead.

Bé rubbed her forehead. Her scar didn't hurt, but it still reminded her of where she'd been.

Bé scribbled on her notepad, "I don't want to go in there."

Ngân said, "I don't either."

*Will we be prisoners here?* Bé wondered.

## CHAPTER 32

Bé GRABBED Ngân's free hand, ready to run, but before the girls could slip away, the guard pulled them inside the orphanage walls. Mèo squeaked from under his bundle but didn't budge from Ngân's grasp. The nun was waiting for them inside as the gate clanged shut behind them, the sound making them both jump. Bé looked at the closed gate, at the city behind it, at the freedom she had lost again.

"Come on," the nun said.

She led the girls through an empty courtyard lined with trees and benches, and into a small administrative building. Ngân clutched Mèo and the bundle of clothes tight to her chest, hiding him from view of the grown-ups who passed in the hallway. The tiled floor was faded and the yellow paint on the walls was peeling, but Bé recognized the cross on the wall. It was just like the one on the rosary that Cô Huệ had given her. *Hope for the impossible.*

The nun led the girls into a large office. A plaque by the door read "Mother Superior's Office."

In the corner of the room, an old nun sat behind a big desk. She was clad in all white, from the headdress hiding her hair to the bottom of her long gown. She had deep wrinkles and sunken eyes behind round glasses. *She looks like she's a hundred years old,* Bé thought.

The two girls looked at each other nervously.

"Mother Superior," said the nun who had escorted them inside. "These are the two little girls from the hospital. The administrators say they are orphans."

*Orphans.* The word felt wrong and sent shivers through Bé. *I'm not an orphan. We'll only be here until Ba comes.*

"The younger girl claims they have a father who is alive. Word has been sent to him, but he hasn't responded."

The older nun nodded. She turned and gave the two girls a stern glance. "Welcome, girls, to our orphanage. Sister Bernadette, here, will escort you to the dormitories, and Sister Lucia will give you a tour around the orphanage later. Be polite and listen to their instructions. Sister Lucia will be your sister in charge from now on." Mother Superior's voice was cold and very matter-of-fact.

Mother Superior flicked her hand, and Sister Bernadette ushered the girls back out of the room and through the building. They walked along a short outdoor pathway that led to a small metal gate. Children peered through the gate, fingers clutching the poles. Their eyes were curious, some a little sad. Some looked friendly; others frowned.

*Is an orphanage a prison for children? Will I ever be truly free again?*

Sister Bernadette unlocked the gate and nudged Bé and Ngân into a large dirt courtyard teeming with children. She entered the courtyard as well, making sure the gate was secure. Four tall buildings loomed in front of them.

Bé and Ngân stood frozen together. The orphanage was overcrowded with girls of all ages. A group squatted together on the ground playing marbles. Others sat on branches of trees that were planted at various locations throughout the yard. There were girls playing hopscotch and jumping rope. A few sat on the steps of the buildings, eyes sullen and haunted.

Bé felt overwhelmed. She had never been around so many children her age. Even when she had gone to school, her village had been small, with only thirty children in her entire grade.

Mèo wriggled free from underneath the pile of clothes where he'd been hiding and jumped down to the ground. The keys dangling from Sister Bernadette's waist seemed to catch his attention, and he reached for them, swatting where they hung.

She shooed Mèo away. "Stop it." She scowled. "Wait, where'd this cat come from?"

Two girls ran toward the nearest building, chanting, "Sister Lucia! Sister Lucia!"

Another girl with pigtails yelled, "We have guests! New girls!"

"Wait here," Sister Bernadette told Bé and Ngân, before following the girl with pigtails toward the building.

A cluster of curious kids surrounded the two girls like bees swarming a hive.

"Hey, a cat!" a girl with long hair said, pointing to Mèo. "Is it yours?"

Mèo hobbled over to the girl, who affectionately petted his back.

"What happened to its paw?" asked a scowly faced girl, her eyebrows knit so tightly together that Bé wanted to run her fingers over them and smooth out the frown lines. She reminded her of Cô Bích, and the memory pricked at her eyes.

"Did its paw get blown off in an explosion?" asked the girl with long hair.

Bé shook her head and squatted down on the ground next to her cat, giving him a scratch behind his ears. His soft fur against her fingertips sent a warm tingle through her. Mèo always made her feel better.

"We think maybe a dog took a bite out of him when he was a baby," Ngân said.

Bé nodded.

"I think he's super cute with his hobble, and he gets around with no problem, even with only three paws," Ngân said.

"Don't let Sister Lucia see you with him. She says cats are bad luck," said the scowly girl.

*Just like Big Mother*, Bé thought. *Will Sister Lucia be cruel like my stepmother?* Bé shuddered.

Mèo rubbed his body against the scowly girl, and her face softened a little. He then allowed other kids to pet him, purring as he went in and around their legs. He liked the attention, but then he got bored and sauntered away to a nearby tree.

Soon after, a middle-aged nun was walking toward them with Sister Bernadette. They wore matching white habits.

"Hello, children, I am Sister Lucia," the middle-aged nun said as she reached them. She scanned some papers in her hands. She and Sister Bernadette bowed to one another, hands clasped together, and the younger nun left, heading toward the courtyard's exit. "Follow me, girls."

*Sister Lucia doesn't seem mean*, Bé thought. Her face was soft, her voice kind. Bé felt a little better.

Ngân and Bé waved their goodbyes to the group of kids and followed Sister Lucia into one of the four buildings.

"The hospital says you are sisters. How old are the two of you?"

"I am thirteen, and my sister is eleven," Ngân said.

The girls held hands as they entered a long corridor lined with closed doors on both sides. A large window was open at the end of the hall, letting in the sunlight, but the hallway was still bathed in shadow. It made the hairs on Bé's arms perk up.

"You'll have good company here. The children I care for have all lost their families, whether through death or other life hardships, just like you," Sister Lucia explained.

Bé slowed, thinking about the children in the courtyard. They had lost their parents, too. She and Ngân were like them. Ngân's parents were dead. And Bé had been separated from hers.

"Keep up, girls," Sister Lucia said. "Your father

has a month to come to retrieve you. If he does not come by the end of the month, you'll be available for adoption."

*Available for adoption?* This scared Bé. *If Ba doesn't come, will we be adopted together, or will they separate us?* Bé couldn't bear the thought.

"There are lots of families who need girls your age to work as servants in their homes, washing and cooking and mending. We try to adopt our children to kind families who treat them well, but unfortunately that doesn't always happen," Sister Lucia continued.

Bé gripped the rosary she wore as a necklace. *Ba has to come. Everything depends on it.*

Sister Lucia stopped at an open door to a classroom. A chalkboard hung on the wall, and wooden desks and chairs were tucked neatly under the desks. "The younger sister will take her classes here."

They passed more classrooms, and then entered a very large room with many long tables and stacks of clean bowls and chopsticks in the center of each table. "This is the refectory, where you will take your meals. Upstairs are the dormitories, where you will sleep.

Tonight, one of the sisters will be around to help you get adjusted, and tomorrow you'll start your classes."

Sister Lucia then led them up a flight of stairs. "The dormitories are separated by age. The younger sister will stay here," Sister Lucia ushered the girls into an excessively large room with rows and rows of rattan cots lined up next to one another. "The older sister will be housed in the building next door."

*Wait . . . what?* Bé clutched at Ngân's hand, eyes frantic.

"You don't understand—my sister and I have to stay together. I . . . I don't want to leave her," Ngân protested.

"You're both safe now. You'll see each other on Sundays at mass, and during the free time afterward."

They'd be separated, and only get to see each other on Sundays. *Only one day a week!* Bé started to hyperventilate.

"But . . . But . . . ," Ngân stammered.

Ngân was all Bé had left. *I won't be separated from my friend. No, never again!*

"No," Ngân screamed. "You don't understand. We. Stay. Together."

Bé crumbled down on the floor. She wanted all of this to go away, for grown-ups to stop controlling their lives.

In the end, after Ngân wouldn't stop screaming and Bé wouldn't stop shaking, Sister Lucia relented, and the girls were allowed to sleep in the same room.

But only for the next thirty days.

# CHAPTER 33

Bé SHIVERED under her blanket. She wrapped it around her body like a cocoon, but she couldn't get warm. Everything was cold—from the rattan mat to the lumpy pillow to the scratchy blanket. It was a humid night, but Bé felt like there were icicles on her skin. She sat up and peeked out underneath the mosquito net that covered her cot.

All was silent. The windowless room was filled with rows and rows of children sleeping peacefully on their cots while Bé's head spun. Even Ngân was sleeping peacefully.

*How can she sleep at a time like this? We're prisoners and, in a month, she'll be moved to another building and possibly adopted . . . unless Ba comes. How do I convince him to take Ngân?*

Bé wished Mèo was there, but there were no windows for him to sneak into the room and find her. She clutched her blanket, worried that he'd be lost to her again, but a deep part inside her knew he was outside waiting for her like he had been at the hospital.

At some point, Bé fell asleep, because a loud bell woke her with a start. Then a high-pitched voice began to chant, "In the name of the Father, Son, and Holy Spirit."

It was still dark outside, but the lights in the dormitory were turned on. All the girls in the room jumped out of bed and knelt on the floor. In unison, they chanted the same words. *They must be prayers*, Bé thought. She didn't know any Catholic prayers. Má hadn't taught her, and her family didn't worship anyone but the ancestors. She turned to see that Ngân looked confused as well.

When the prayer was finished, the girls began to talk to one another.

A young nun by the door yelled, "Let's get ready for

mass, then to classes. Now make your bed, go to the lavatory, wash your face, and brush your teeth."

Each girl neatly arranged her bed. Mosquito nets were lifted and the fabric tucked on top. Blankets were folded into squares and placed at the center of each bed, the pillow on top.

Bé felt heavy and lay back down. Ngân went over to her and felt her forehead. "You're burning up."

"My sister is sick," Ngân said to the nun by the door.

The nun came to them and felt Bé's forehead and said, "To the infirmary with her. But you, go to your classes."

Bé didn't want Ngân to go, and neither did Ngân. "I need to stay with her."

"Go to classes. We will take care of her," the nun snapped, and pushed Ngân toward the lavatory.

Once in the infirmary, a nurse gave Bé pills to reduce her fever, and she was given permission to take the rest of the day off from classes. She retreated into the safety of sleep.

She dreamed of Xuân. He was in a dense forest, trying to find her. Darkness surrounded him, and she could hear the slither of snakes hissing.

"Little Sister, where are you?" he called.

She opened her mouth, but no words came. Instead, moths flew out of her mouth and fluttered away. She jumped to catch them, but they were too quick and disappeared. Her brother took off another way. She tried to follow him, but her legs were mush and she collapsed onto the forest floor. She crawled on her stomach, but then snakes began to slither around her body, curling and squeezing. She couldn't breathe. She was screaming, and then . . .

"Friend, it's okay. It's only a nightmare." It was Ngân's voice.

She opened her eyes to find Ngân sitting by her side. They were alone in the dormitory. Bé sat up and leaned against her friend. It was dark, but a single light illuminated the room enough for them to see each other.

"They're eating dinner, but I was given permission to come eat with you," Ngân said. She stood up and retrieved a large, round platter with food from a nearby table. There were two large bowls of rice, bitter melon soup, and chargrilled fish with fish sauce for dipping. The food looked and smelled good. Not as good as Cô

Huệ's but much better than what they were fed underground, or what Big Mother forced her to eat when she was home.

Bé was ravenous and ate quickly. Ngân giggled, wiping her mouth with the back of her hand. Bé grinned. As long as Ngân was with her, she knew she would be okay.

"Your father will come," Ngân said quietly, as they finished their meal.

Bé took out her notebook. "We stay together. No matter what," she wrote.

Ngân didn't say anything. She gathered the dirty dishes and returned them to the table. "I'm going to check on Mèo. He found a tree to hide in."

Bé smiled, happy to know her cat was safe.

The nuns kept the children on a strict routine—mass, then breakfast, then class, followed by outside time and lunch, then class until dinner. The lights turned off at eight at night and the day began again before daybreak.

The sisters taught the girls writing and reading, mathematics, science, history, geography, and other basic subjects. Bé and Ngân soon became accustomed to daily life in the orphanage.

Bé sat next to a girl named Linh, whose face had been burned by a flamethrower, and whose parents died in the same attack that had sent her and Ngân to the hospital. Linh didn't say much, but once, when she caught Bé staring at her burns, she let Bé feel the rough patches on her skin.

"It doesn't hurt anymore," Linh said.

*We are all broken*, Bé thought.

Bé and Ngân were in different classes, so they only saw each other during mealtimes and during the outside time before lunch. They made new friends with the other orphans, but they still clung to each other the way real sisters would.

When they were outside, they played with Mèo, who was getting bigger with each passing day. Mèo stayed in a large jackfruit tree near the dormitory buildings, perching on a low branch until he saw one of the girls. Then he'd climb down to greet them.

Sometimes Mèo disappeared for days at a time, which made the girls worry at first, but he always returned, looking fatter than before. Bé's stomach was in knots during these disappearances, always nervous that he wouldn't come back, or that something would happen to him when he was gone, but when he came back, he'd always come to her first and let her squeeze him for as long as she needed.

One afternoon, the girls sat giving him all the attention he craved. "He must be going to visit Cô Huệ," Ngân told Bé. "He's filling out fast. Look at his cute chubby tummy. His fur is looking cleaner and healthier, too. Do you think she's been giving him baths?"

Bé shrugged, rubbing Mèo's belly as he purred. She smiled, thinking of the fight he'd probably put up during a bath.

# CHAPTER 34

Bé COUNTED the days that passed at the orphanage, knowing that her time with Ngân was short. Bé wanted to find ways to escape, just in case her father never came, but she hadn't figured it out. There were safeguards—gates and buildings and guards—at the orphanage to keep the children in. It wasn't even possible to go to the exterior courtyard, where the gate was that led out to the city. You had to go through the Mother Superior's office building to reach it, and then there were the locked gates and the guard manning it.

Still, Bé walked along the fence of the interior court-yard, feeling it for any weak spots. Mèo always trailed behind, keeping her company. *The fence is too high to climb*, Bé decided, *and the bars are too close together.* Scaling the trees wouldn't work as an escape either. They were planted too far away. It was hopeless.

As the month deadline loomed, Bé began to lose her appetite. Her stomach stayed in knots, and she'd bitten her nails to the quick. But two days before the deadline, Sister Lucia found the two girls jumping rope with Linh and her friends.

"You have some visitors," Sister Lucia said. "They're waiting for you in the front courtyard."

*Could it be?* Bé prayed for the impossible. *Please let it be Ba.*

Bé clutched Ngân's hand, and the two girls followed Sister Lucia down the path to the other side of the gate, through Mother Superior's office, to the exterior courtyard.

Two figures—a skeletal man and a beanstalk of a boy—were sitting on a bench under a tall, shady tree. Bé recognized them at once.

Ba and Xuân.

Bé couldn't believe her eyes. Her heart leaped. She bounded toward them, arms spread wide.

Her father was frail, weaker than he had ever been. He leaned heavily on Xuân for support. Her brother had grown taller, but he'd lost weight. His cheeks were gaunt, and his face was marred with new scars and bruises. *Big Mother*, Bé thought unhappily.

She reached them and wrapped her arms around Ba. Tears burst from her eyes, and their eyes were wet too. Ba took her face in his hands and kissed her on the forehead and both cheeks.

Ngân stood awkwardly behind, while Mother Superior waited by the front door of the building.

"Are you well, con?" Ba asked, the worry resounding off every syllable. She nodded and embraced him again, holding on tightly, not wanting to let go.

"Praise to Buddha you are unharmed. After I learned what happened . . . I did not know . . . I did not know . . . Forgive me, my child." Ba wept, his face stricken with grief. He clutched her to him, and she cried in his arms.

Her heart felt full. For a moment, she forgot about the underground bunker, the terrible men, the war, and Cô Lan and her friends who may have died trying to save her. She didn't want to let him go. She wanted to stay in this moment forever.

Ba was the first to let go. "I should have protected you. I have failed you as a father." His face contorted into the most sorrowful expression.

Bé wanted to tell him, "I forgive you, Ba." She opened her mouth to do so, but the words stuck in the back of her throat.

"I need to talk to the Mother Superior," Ba said, looking beyond her.

She didn't want to be apart from him for another second. She grabbed his hand, and he squeezed it once before letting it go.

"Stay here with Xuân," he said.

As she watched him walk away, her heart sank.

Xuân put his hand on her shoulder, and she hugged him so hard that he exclaimed, "My ribs! My ribs hurt!" He laughed and then tousled her hair, like he had when they were younger.

She reached out and touched the green bruise on his cheek.

"I'm glad you are safe from her now . . . I will

never forgive her for what she made me do." The regret in his voice was thick as he ran a finger over her forehead.

She wanted to tell him she forgave him. "Xxx . . . ," her mouth said, making a strange sound, but the words wouldn't come.

"You are safer here with these nuns," Xuân whispered in her ear, pulling her to him and squeezing hard. "If you go home, Mother will only take her temper out on you. I am stronger, and I can bear it. She is my mother. She will not go as far with me, but you . . . we don't want this future for you, Little Sister."

*What?*

"You are to stay here," Xuân said, releasing her. His face was crestfallen, and his lips curled in a frown. "We wanted to see you one last time. We wanted to make sure you were well. We love you too much. I will miss you."

*They're leaving me?*

*NO!* This. Can. Not. Be. Happening.

This isn't happening.

She looked for her notepad and pencil, but she had

left them inside. She wrapped her arms tight around Xuân's chest, willing him to take her, letting the tears fall. She sobbed, hiccupping.

*Don't leave me! Stay with me.*

She tried to make the sound "*Nooooo*," but again, her voice was strangled, like an injured animal. Her vocal chords caved in, collapsing, refusing to work when she desperately needed them to cooperate.

Ngân grabbed one of her hands.

"I'm sorry, con," Ba said, coming to stand next to Ngân. His voice cracked, and she saw the tears in his eyes. "My sweet child."

"B-b . . . a," Bé rasped, the word caught in her throat, choking her, as the tears refused to stop. She was tired of crying, tired of saying goodbye to the people she loved most in the world.

Her father looked pained, the corners of his mouth upturned, his jaw trembling. He hugged her one last time, then patted her shoulder and leaned on Xuân for support. Slowly, the two of them walked away toward the front gate.

They didn't look back.

A strangled, keening wail, shrill and high in pitch, escaped Bé's lips.

She didn't understand. *Why is this happening? How can this happen? He is my blood. He is my father. He's supposed to protect me. He isn't supposed to leave. He is supposed to look back.*

Bé felt Ngân's and Sister Lucia's eyes on her, felt their pity.

*No. I am not an orphan.*

Realization crashed around her like a tidal wave crushing a sand dune. Without Ba, Ngân would be sent to the other dormitory, and she would be left alone. Without anyone.

*Hope . . . hope for the impossible . . .*

She had held onto that ridiculous wish for so long. But it had never been real, just pretty words a priest had once told her to get her to leave the forest and return home.

The guard was pushing the gate closed and, without another thought, Bé made a break for it, pulling Ngân with her.

The guard at the gate stopped the girls, easily

grabbing them. Bé kicked and thrashed, but the guard was too strong.

"B-b-a!" Bé tried to say again, the word tangling in her throat, sounding more like a wheeze than anything.

Down the street, Bé could see Ba and Xuân stepping onto a crowded bus, and she watched in horror as the bus lurched away.

*Just like Má.*

"They're gone," Ngân said beside her.

*Gone.*

They were gone.

She would never see Ba or Xuân again. Though she wanted to squash the thought as quickly as it came, the truth hit her like the mortar explosion had done, throwing her into the air. As if it was happening all over again, she saw her body slam against the rice paddy fields. She saw her best friend bleeding.

Bé wailed, her throat raw from the effort of trying to speak. She clutched the bars of the gate. Ngân hugged her, rocking her back and forth like Cô Lan had rocked Tuyết on the nights when she was having a particularly bad episode.

"It's okay . . . I'm here . . . You're okay." Ngân's voice sounded grown up, so much like Cô Lan's, and this made Bé cry even harder. Her friend—no, her sister, the only family she had left, the only person to love her— shouldn't have to comfort her like this. They should be like the other kids, playing and laughing, not having to shoulder the burden of their families selling them, fathers and mothers abandoning them, of losing women who loved and protected them to evil men and the war.

Soft fur tickled Bé's ankles. Mèo had jumped down from his tree and was purring, rubbing his body against her leg. Bé clutched Mèo to her chest. He was the only thing she had left of home.

## CHAPTER 35

Bé sat on the ground by the gates of the dormitory courtyard where everyone played each day. She couldn't stop crying. She clutched the bars of her prison so hard that it was leaving marks on her skin. Ngân sat next to her friend, rubbing her back, trying to offer what little comfort she could. Ngân was shaking, too.

It was dinnertime now, and everyone was inside but the girls.

"You may stay outside, but just for tonight. Tomorrow, Ngân will have to move to the other dormitory," Sister Lucia had said, her voice soft and full of sympathy.

*Tomorrow, they're taking Ngân away*, Bé thought as she sobbed. *What will I do without her?*

Mèo was on the other side of the gate, jumping up and down, swatting something metallic that clinked against the metal bars. Bé could barely see through her tears and the dimming light. Daylight was fading fast.

Mèo's claws stuck on something jingly in the dirt. Then he swatted and pawed it closer to the girls. He squeaked as he played with a little bounce in his step.

Bé sniffed. Mèo always liked playing with things that made noise.

Ngân said, "Wish we were as carefree as he is."

Bè pulled her notepad and pencil out of her pocket and wrote, "What are we going to do?"

"I don't know." Ngân frowned and bit her lip.

Mèo pounced on the object, his claws extending and scratching the bottom of the metal bars with an annoying screech. It hurt Bé's ears.

The setting sun reflected off the metallic object. *Is that . . . ?*

Mèo was playing with a set of keys attached to a chain.

*It can't be . . .* Bé reached her hand through the gate, picked up the keys, and showed them to Ngân. Her eyes widened.

"Do you think . . . ?"

Bé nodded. *How did Mèo get ahold of them?* She then remembered how he had swiped at Sister Bernadette's keys more than once in the courtyard, and how he'd always managed to escape before she could catch him. Mèo was a great escape artist.

"Try and see if it fits," Ngân said. She looked around them. "Do it before the nuns come and get us."

The girls stood. Bé put her notepad back in her pocket and easily slid her skinny arm through the holes in the gate. She stuck out her tongue as she stretched her arm around to put one of the keys into the lock.

*Click.* The key turned and the gate slowly swung open.

Ngân grabbed Mèo and the girls ran down the path to Mother Superior's office.

The key that unlocked the courtyard gate did not unlock the administrative building. Bé fumbled as she tried the different keys on the keychain. Her heart was pounding so loudly that she was worried the world could hear it. Her fingers were sweaty. Long minutes passed before she found a key that worked.

The inside of the building was dark. The lights were off. No one was inside.

The girls ran through the long hallway as fast as they could. Mèo made an annoyed sound in Ngân's arms, but he didn't try to jump down.

The girls had been in the building only hours before, and Bé followed the same path to the door that led to the exterior courtyard.

Ngân peeked out the door to see if there was anyone in the courtyard. She made a motion with her head for Bé to follow. The girls closed the door as quietly as they could and tiptoed toward the front gate. They hid behind a bench to locate the orphanage guard.

*Please don't see us*, Bé thought. Thankfully, the guard was across the street talking to an attractive lady at a food cart. He was touching her arm, and she was giggling. The girls waited until his back was turned to them and made a dash for the gate.

Once there, Bé's arms shook as she tried the keys in the lock. She put in the first key. Nothing. The guard was still turned. She chose another key. *Please work.*

*Click.*

Relief flooded Bé, her heart pounding.

The girls took off away from where the guard stood. They bumped into a man, who cursed loudly. Then they heard someone else yell, "STOP!"

Bé turned to see the guard heading their way. Bé and Ngân ran as fast as their legs could carry them, and they soon escaped into the city.

PART 5

# A NEW NAME

## CHAPTER 36

LEFT, LEFT, RIGHT, LEFT. The girls zigzagged, running into busy streets jam-packed with vendors, bicycles, motorbikes, and people. Bé's side cramped, but she forced her legs to keep going. Ngân stumbled, panting. Finally, the two girls ducked into a dark alleyway to stop and catch their breath. Ngân, who had been clutching Mèo the entire time, let the cat down. Mèo let out an unhappy mew and began to groom himself.

Bé peeked out around the corner back into the street. No guard. The girls had lost him among the throngs of people in the city.

Bé felt hollow, like she was a fish with its insides gutted. But they were free. For the first time in months, they could go anywhere they wanted. No locked rooms, no fences that kept them in. Bé pulled the rosary from her neck, snapping it like Big Mother had done. She threw it on the ground. *Hoping for the impossible is pointless.* All it had done was make things worse. She would make her own future.

Bé pulled out her notepad and wrote, "We're free."

"Should we try to find Cô Huệ? I bet she will help us," Ngân asked.

Bé thought about this, but then shook her head. *Grown-ups are not to be trusted.* Má had left her to Big Mother, who sold her. The scary men had imprisoned her. The orphanage was going to separate her and Ngân, and her father had decided to abandon her forever. No, trusting adults had only hurt her.

"She might send us back," Bé wrote.

"I don't want to go back either," Ngân said.

Bé didn't know where to go from there, so she chose a direction and walked ahead. *We have each other and we'll make it on our own.*

The girls and their three-footed cat wandered aimlessly for several hours. An angry man lugging a metal food cart yelled for the girls to get out of his way. The scent of roasted quail wafted in the air. Bé's mouth watered, remembering the taste of meat.

"I'm hungry," Ngân said.

Exhausted from walking, the girls decided to ask for money to get something to eat. They squatted and held palms outstretched to passersby. Bé grunted whenever anyone came near, and Ngân begged, "Please. Some đồng so we can eat."

A man tossed them one đồng, not enough money to buy even a loaf of bread. Ngân tucked it in her pocket, and they walked from street to street, begging.

A woman carrying two overflowing baskets of produce handed them a yellow pomelo fruit from her basket. They tore into the sweet, large grapefruit and ate it hungrily.

By the time that the streets emptied, both girls were dusty and dirty, but they had enough money to buy a meat bánh mì sandwich from a vendor closing for the night. They ate it slowly, allowing the flavors of sweet and sour to linger on their tongues. As night fell, they found a small space between two buildings to sleep.

Mèo curled up on Bé's chest like he had when he was a kitten—when their lives were very different. *You're almost a fully grown cat now, not my tiny kitten anymore.* Mèo felt very heavy on her chest, but Bé ignored the discomfort and smiled as she fell asleep, thinking, *I'm free.*

The girls spent the next day like the one before, wandering from street to street with Mèo sticking close by them, having no destination in mind, approaching people and asking for spare đồng, enough for them to buy something to eat. And for another night, they slept again down a quiet alley.

The third day, they woke to rain. They found shelter underneath an awning and drank the rainwater. That evening they slept between the bodies of other homeless people. There were many people displaced by the war, homes destroyed and with nothing left.

Each day took on the same rhythm: beg, eat, sleep. Mèo disappeared from time to time, but he always returned. As the girls became hungrier and hungrier, Ngân began to bat at things that weren't there. Her eyes would stare unblinkingly, and she swayed like a twig in the wind. Sometimes she mumbled incoherently. Bé, too, felt weak, and her thirst made it hard to focus and see straight.

On a particularly bleak morning, as they stood on a new corner for begging, Ngân crumbled to the ground. They had been unlucky begging for several days, and it had been a day and a half since they had last eaten. "I can't walk anymore," Ngân said. "I'm hungry. I'm thirsty. My feet hurt." She was out of breath and was pale as a ghost. She could barely hold her head up. "I can't . . . anymore."

Bé didn't know what to do. Ngân wouldn't last much longer without food, and if they went back, they'd be separated, probably adopted to different families, and she'd never see Ngân again. But she didn't want Ngân to die either.

A church bell rang in the distance, and Mèo ran off ahead, following the sound.

Bé remembered Cô Huệ saying she lived near the

cathedral. *Should I try to find Cô Huệ for help? But what if she sends us back to the orphanage?*

Ngân's eyelids were starting to droop. Bé draped Ngân's arms around her shoulder and hoisted her up. Bé was wobbly and her muscles weak, but she steeled herself. She had to find Cô Huệ. Even if she sent them back to the orphanage, at least she could feed them. And at least Ngân would not die. Cô Huệ had said she would help.

*Mèo knows where she lives. We just have to follow him.* She could do this. She had to do this. If she didn't, Ngân could die.

Bé dragged Ngân toward the sound of the bell, following their cat. They headed into a crowded street, and Bé saw a man selling nước mía. She grabbed her notebook and wrote, "Church."

"You mean, the cathedral?" the man asked, and Bé nodded enthusiastically. The man gave her directions and then handed her a bag of fresh sugarcane juice.

Bé bowed to thank him. She took a few sips and guided the straw to Ngân's mouth, urging her to drink.

Ngân sipped, slowly at first and then faster until the

bag was almost empty. Bé sucked the rest of the juice down.

With her thirst quenched, Ngân seemed more awake, but Bé still had to help support her. After a ten-minute walk from the sugarcane stall, they reached the base of the hill where the cathedral stood. They stopped to catch their breath. Bé's shoulder ached from carrying most of Ngân's weight. Ngân's cheeks had more color in them, but she still looked sick.

Bé pulled out her notepad and wrote, "We're going to find Cô Huệ's house."

"How?" Ngân asked. "We don't know where she lives."

"Mèo does," Bé wrote.

Bé looked around for Mèo, but he had disappeared. She panicked. She didn't know what to do. *Should I leave Ngân here to wait while I search for Mèo?*

"Let's go up to the church," Bé wrote.

Ngân nodded and followed.

The girls made their way up a set of cracked concrete steps that led to the massive church. Bé found a discarded bánh bao on one of the steps, half eaten, and tore it in half. They each ate their part as they climbed.

At the top, they could see the entire city. Tiny square buildings and tiled roofs were spread out, speckled with green trees. In the distance, there were mountains and the sky was a rich blue. Bé was mesmerized by the sight.

All of a sudden, Ngân tugged Bé down a very narrow set of steps that were chipped and uneven. They were descending too fast, and Bé nearly tripped and fell.

"He found us," Ngân said, frantic, her eyes wild.

Bé looked over her shoulder. There was no one there. Only chipped steps, and the church behind it. Ngân was delirious.

"He's following!" Ngân screamed.

Bé stopped her friend. "Who?" she wrote on her notepad.

"It's the old man!" Ngân said, pulling them again through a maze of narrow alleys between a row of homes. "He's found us. He's going to take us back."

## CHAPTER 37

Bé GRABBED HER FRIEND and hugged her with all her might. Ngân calmed. She looked around. The person she had been running from had seemingly disappeared.

The girls were standing between houses in a small neighborhood. Each home was connected to the next by a single wall, their doors and windows open showing their occupants. People looked at the girls quizzically as they passed. Bé didn't know where to go next, but at least Ngân's grip on her hand was tight.

She kept her eyes peeled for Mèo. *If Cô Huệ lives near the cathedral, we must be close.*

They arrived at a set of train tracks. The deafening horn of an oncoming train blared, and they waited for it to pass before crossing. Then they rounded a corner and squeezed into the space between two buildings, crossing into another neighborhood.

A cat with familiar stripes ran into one of the houses.

Three feet. Striped, gray fur.

"Mèo!" Ngân yelled.

The cat mewed from inside. Bé's heart skipped a beat. She wanted to cry.

The cat poked its head out of the doorway, looked at the girls, and then disappeared back inside. Ngân dropped Bé's hand and had a terrified expression on her face. Her eyes grew wild. *I have to help Ngân*, Bé thought. *Now.*

Bé grabbed Ngân's hand again and pulled her straight into the house after the cat.

Someone hummed in the next room as something sizzled. The humming stopped. Bé froze. They had walked into a stranger's home—a stranger who might be dangerous. The girls needed to hide. Grown-ups were not to be trusted. Grown-ups abandoned you. They sold you. They aimed guns at you. They made you orphans.

Bé looked around the small room. An altar was set

up against the wall where a cross hung, and framed black-and-white photos were displayed on a table next to a bowl of fruit. There was an empty bed pushed against the corner. Next to that was a wood ladder leading upstairs.

She quickly pulled Ngân toward the bed, and they dove underneath.

Another train rumbled past, and everything trembled. The aroma of rice and fried shrimp wafted in the air. Bé's stomach groaned loudly, but the chug-chug of the loud train muffled the sound.

"Is he coming?" Ngân asked. "Will he take us back to the bunker?"

Bé put her finger over her mouth. She needed Ngân to stop talking or else they would get caught. Bé's mind raced with worry. *What do they do with runaways? Will they send us back to the orphanage, or will they turn us in to the police? Is this city controlled by the Việt Cộng or the South Vietnamese Army?*

When the train passed, all was quiet in the house. Ngân and Bé stayed in their hiding spot. They heard movement in the next room—the kitchen. Voices. A man's and a woman's. Ngân pressed her hand over her mouth; her body was trembling.

Time slowed to a crawl. A second passed. Another heartbeat. Another second.

Bé had been afraid for so long—of Big Mother, of dark holes underground, men with big guns . . . She was tired of running, tired of being afraid.

Movement distracted her from her thoughts. Someone was coming.

Feet stepped into the room—petite feet, followed by larger ones.

"They're here. I saw them enter your home." A man's voice. He was young and wore boots. Soldier's boots.

*Had Ngân seen him earlier and confused him with the old man? Is he a good soldier or a bad one?*

"Hoàng, there's no one here. I think you've been working too hard."

Another voice—a woman. Bé thought she recognized the voice.

*Cô Huệ?* Bé couldn't be certain.

"Má! I'm not seeing things." It was the soldier's voice again. He scared her. *We'll have to wait until he's gone,* Bé thought.

The woman spoke again. "Come, why don't you take a break from patrolling and have some early dinner with me?"

The voice did sound exactly like Co Huệ. *Had Mèo led them to Cô Huệ's house?*

*Of course he would*, Bé thought with a smile. She squeezed Ngân's hand.

Her beloved cat had comforted her, loved her when she was scared and alone. He had saved her from the orphanage, and now he had led her to Cô Huệ, who had cared for her in the hospital when she'd had no one else.

Doubt crept in. *What if Cô Huệ is just as bad as Big Mother in the real world? What if it's all been a lie? Is the soldier her son?* Bé didn't know what to do.

"I'm going to look upstairs," he said. His footsteps retreated, clomping up the stairs.

The woman entered the room fully, sat down on the bed, and sighed. The weight of her body pushed the mattress down. Ngân and Bé flattened their bodies to the ground.

The church bell chimed. Then came the sweet sound of a cat mewing.

"Oh, cat. Where have you been?"

Mèo scrambled underneath the bed. He purred as he rubbed his sides against Bé's face. He was making too much noise.

The woman's face popped sharply into view, her nose inches from Bé's face. It was Cô Huệ.

Ngân screamed.

Bé froze.

Cô Huệ's eyes enlarged at the sight of the two girls. "OUT!"

They scrambled out from their hiding spots. Then the soldier came down the stairs.

"Caught you!" His voice was triumphant.

Ngân screamed again, while Bé's jaw trembled. She thought of that dark, terrible place and all the stories her brother had told her about the Việt Cộng soldiers. She couldn't stop herself. She wet herself.

The girls stumbled backward, away from the man.

"What's going on?" Cô Huệ said. "Hoàng, you are scaring the girls! And girls, why aren't you at the orphanage?"

Bé stared between Cô Huệ and the soldier. There was nowhere she could go where the monsters wouldn't find her. Men were dangerous. But she was so tired of being afraid. She needed to be safe, and Ngân needed her to be strong.

She remembered Ba's words. *Have strength*, he'd said. *You have more strength in you than steel, and the courage of a leopard.*

Then she thought of Má. *You must be brave for me now*, she'd said.

Bé swallowed.

She grabbed Ngân's hand, but Ngân was holding something. Smooth, round beads. Bé looked down to see the rosary she had thrown away. Ngân had saved it.

Méo purred and rubbed his head against Bé's leg.

Bé took a deep breath and said . . . "P-please."

She forced the air out of her lungs. She forced her voice to work. Everything depended on her. She had to find her voice. She had to save her friend.

"Don't . . . let . . . him . . . take us. Let us stay."

Cô Huệ embraced the girls at once and said, "Tell me everything."

# CHAPTER 38

## Twelve Months Later

Ngân and her sister held up glowing paper lanterns and cheered with the other neighborhood children as they watched the múa lân—the unicorn dance for the Mid-Autumn Festival. A man danced around with a pot-belly and plastic mask, playing the part of Ông Địa, the spirit of the earth. He wore a red and gold áo dài outfit and fanned himself, dancing around merrily. He feigned giggling, his hand to his mouth as two men wearing the unicorn outfit kicked and jumped, the unicorn head bouncing down and up to the rhythm of the drums and cymbals that the men in the back played. There were teenage boys doing kung-fu and karate moves as part of the parade.

"Do you remember Cô Lan telling us that her father played Ông Địa one year?" Ngân asked.

"Yes! And he tore his áo dài when he leaned over because he'd gotten too fat, eating too much coconut candy," giggled Hiếu—once called Bé, and before that, Thương.

Cô Huệ had officially adopted the girls and given Bé a new name. The best name she could have hoped for.

"Hiếu."

A name that meant honor and faithfulness to your family.

Hiếu's sad memories hurt less and less the longer time went on, and she liked to remember the women who had saved her.

Hiếu held up her lantern. It was a red lotus, and Ngân's was a yellow butterfly. Surrounding the girls were illuminated lanterns in star patterns, fish, and dragons. Hiếu looked at her sister and beamed, showing all her teeth, her stomach full of sweet moon cake and sticky rice cake.

"Your butterfly is prettier than my lotus," Hiếu said. "Next year, I want a dragon lantern."

"I want a fish one," Ngân said. "Remember when I wanted to be a fisherwoman on the Mê Kông?"

"But you get seasick in boats!" Hiếu said.

The girls giggled, their laughter soon drowned out by the claps, hoots, and excited hollers from the crowd. Méo frolicked nearby, never straying too far from the girls.

Hiếu never thought she could ever feel happiness again, but there she was, happy with her new family. Her voice was fully recovered. She loved to sing and talk and talk to anyone who would listen. Her hand was healing better than expected. Even her forehead scar had faded and was now a white-and-flesh-colored mark with just a little hint of green remaining. Her longer, black hair, which Cô Huệ brushed every night like Má had, covered the remnants of it.

These days, Hiếu thought about the dark times of her life only every once in a while. Whenever she thought about Má, she focused on remembering the good memories of life when they were together in their old village, not when they lived with Ba and Big Mother. She wasn't mad at Má anymore, now that she knew the truth.

Hoàng—Hiếu's new older brother, who wasn't such a scary soldier after all—had brought Xuân to see Hiếu last month and also found out what had happened to Má.

After Má left, she'd found a job in Saigon, but it didn't make enough money for her to retrieve Hiếu right away. She spent a year saving the money. Then, while she was on her way back to get Hiếu, her motorbike tripped a landmine, and she died.

Her mother had loved her. She hadn't abandoned her. Hiếu was comforted by this, but she still cried sometimes knowing that her mother was no longer alive, and that she'd never see her again. This left an ache inside Hiếu that she hadn't healed from yet, and maybe she'd never fully heal. But the ache did become less painful as each month passed.

It turned out that Big Mother had known for months that Má had died but kept it a secret until Hiếu was sold. After it was discovered that she'd sold Hiếu behind her husband's back, the village turned their back on her. No one would buy from her at the market. Eventually, Xuân had to take over.

Ba, however, never recovered after he left Hiếu at

the orphanage. Xuân said his heart was too weak and too sad. He died a few weeks after he returned home.

Even though her father had abandoned her, Hiếu still cried and mourned his death. Xuân said that when he grew up, he would move to Hiếu's city, so that they could see each other all the time. Hiếu missed her brother, but she was happy in her new family.

The war had taken so much from her, but it had also given her a new family that loved and cherished her.

"Hiếu! Ngân!" Cô Huệ called from her doorway, not far from where the girls were playing with their lanterns in the street. Hiếu looked back and waved. Cô Huệ was standing by a newly sprouted tamarind tree that had grown spontaneously in the yard. Hiếu couldn't wait until it bore its first fruit.

"Race you home!" Hiếu yelled to Ngân.

And off they went, running home, laughing, their glowing lanterns lighting up the dark.

# AUTHOR'S NOTE

Although I was born in the generation after the Vietnam War ended, I've always been deeply affected by it. All my relatives (my parents, their siblings, my grandparents, and my great-grandparents) lived through the war, and I grew up hearing their stories of what life was like in wartime. Their stories always made me sad, especially knowing the suffering my people went through during that time, and in the years after the war ended.

My very existence is tied to this terrible war, which killed an estimated two million civilians on both sides. If the North Vietnamese communists hadn't won the war, my mother would have continued her schooling as a Catholic nun, and my father would have been a priest. However, when the war broke out, my father joined the South Vietnamese Army, and my mother was sent home to her parents' house. Then, my father spent almost a decade in a "reeducation" camp as a prisoner of war, and they weren't married until after he returned home.

Most novels about the Vietnam War revolve around South Vietnamese refugees fleeing the country after the fall of Saigon, or they are from soldiers' perspectives. These novels are heavily focused on the war after America entered the conflict. However, I wanted to tell a story from a different perspective.

In *Mèo and Bé,* I allude to the death of President Ngô Đình Diệm in 1963, setting *Mèo and Bé* in the spring and summer of 1964. The conversation that Bé's brothers and father have around the lunch table in part two is taken from my father's own opinions after the death of President Ngô Đình Diệm.

I come from a patriotic South Vietnamese family. Like most Vietnamese refugees in America, we are strongly anticommunist and very loyal to our roots. If you go to any Vietnamese gathering, festival, or event in the United States, you will see the South Vietnamese flag—a yellow flag with three red stripes—on proud display. Although this flag is technically defunct (it was the flag of the Republic of South Vietnam, which was overthrown in 1975 when the war ended), it is displayed with pride by the Vietnamese American community. You will never see the official flag of Vietnam, which is red with a yellow star, on display in America. That flag is seen as a symbol of communism and hated by the Vietnamese American community.

Because my roots are South Vietnamese, the Việt Cộng

are seen negatively in this book. They caused a lot of fear among my family members who lived during the war, and they cause fear to the characters in this novel.

However, I didn't intend for *Mèo and Bé* to be a book about the Vietnam War, but about a girl who lives during that time. This is a story about how you can find the light amid the dark. It's a story of courage and never losing hope, even when things seem hopeless. It's a story about finding your voice after you've lost everything.

Although *Mèo and Bé* is a work of fiction, I have weaved some of my family's personal history into this novel. The character of Bé is based on my adopted aunt's life. My Cô Hiếu was the child of a landowner and his concubine. Her mother abandoned her as a young child, and she was mistreated by her father's first wife. The tattoo scene actually happened to my aunt, and she still has a green cross on her forehead from her stepmother's abuse. The Monkey Hill scene also happened, witnessed by my father when he was a solider in the South Vietnamese Army. The character of Cô Huệ is based on my grandmother. My aunt, however, was never sold. What happened to Bé after she was kidnapped and sold is pure fiction. In real life, my aunt was abandoned at a church as a young child, and some of the neighborhood women wanted to raise her to be a slave in their households. My grandmother saved her from that terrible future.

During the Vietnam War, an entire sex industry sprang up around American soldiers stationed in the country. It is not a stretch to imagine that vulnerable women and children were trafficked and held against their will during this chaotic time. Human trafficking is, sadly, a phenomenon that still occurs in Vietnam today. As of 2021, for the third consecutive year, Vietnam was placed on the Tier 2 Watch List from the U.S. Department of State's Office to Monitor and Combat Trafficking in Persons. Previously, Vietnam was ranked Tier 3 (which is the worst ranking). The Tier 2 Watch List means the country "do[es] not fully comply with the Act's minimum standards but are making significant efforts to bring themselves into compliance with those standards, and:

a) The estimated number of victims of severe forms of trafficking is very significant or is significantly increasing and the country is not taking proportional concrete actions; or

b) There is a failure to provide evidence of increasing efforts to combat severe forms of trafficking in persons from the previous year."

The description of the orphanage is based on my father's recollection of living in an orphanage at a young age—he had been placed in an orphanage after my grandfather had been murdered by the Việt Cộng and readopted by his biological mother later in childhood. Bé's home with her father and Big Mother is based on my maternal grandparents' property in South Vietnam, and the cathedral and Cô Huệ's house (with the train tracks) at the very end are based on where my paternal grandmother lived in Vietnam.

The Vietnam War began in 1954 and ended on April 30, 1975, when North Vietnam won the war. The war scarred the landscape of Vietnam. Bombs destroyed roads, railway lines, bridges, and canals. Unexploded shells and landmines were scattered in the countryside, often hidden in the paddy fields. As a result, since the end of the war, 40,000 Vietnamese people have been injured or killed from these hidden explosives. During the war, U.S. forces sprayed more than twenty million gallons of herbicides, including Agent Orange, which destroyed 7,700 square miles of forests. Some 400,000 people were killed or permanently injured, and half a million babies born with birth defects due to exposure to these herbicides. It is also estimated that two million people suffer from cancer and other illnesses due to Agent Orange.

Life in the years after the war was difficult. There was a widespread food shortage, and lots of fear for people who fought for or supported the South Vietnamese Army. The new regime rounded up former South Vietnamese officers and soldiers and sent them to reeducation camps. Later, former government workers and supporters of the old government of South Vietnam were also imprisoned.

Today, Vietnam remains a communist country. The Communist Party has a monopoly on political power, and restricts freedom of expression, opinion, and speech. Anyone who speaks ill of the government is subject to physical harm, harassment, intimidation, and imprisonment. According to Amnesty International, the 2015 Criminal Code criminalizes "making, storing or spreading information, materials or items for the purpose of opposing the State of the Socialist Republic of Viet Nam." The government regularly cracks down on independent journalists, political commentators, bloggers, and anyone who is critical of them.

I keep all of this in mind whenever I go home to visit my family. We are always careful about our conversations and never discuss the communist regime.

The Vietnam War is taught from a different perspective

in Vietnam than we are taught in the United States. For example, the Americans are viewed as foreign invaders and seen as the bad guys.

When I was learning about the Vietnam War in my U.S. high school, I had to learn how to separate the American version from the version my father was telling me at home. They are two different perspectives of the war. Through the years, I've realized that there are always multiple perspectives or points of view to history, depending on who is telling the story. As you, my readers, learn about the Vietnam War, I hope you are able to see the war from the Vietnamese perspective too, not just the American one.

Despite the restrictions on freedom of speech, Vietnam is a beautiful country that has fully recovered from the war. It's grown from one of the poorest countries in the world to a middle income one. Vietnam has become a tourist destination in recent years. It is amazing to visit. The ample paddy fields in the countryside of Vietnam are lush and green. The mountains look magical, like they're out of a fairy tale. The southern beaches have powdery white sand and clear water. The food—especially the street food and the exotic fruits sold in the open air marketplaces—is delicious and fresh. The countryside still retains its charm with old-fashioned country homes, ancient citadels, and pagodas. Ho Chi Minh City (still called Saigon by the locals) looks like any American city with its skyscrapers, chic modern stores, and high-class restaurants.

Vietnam has changed a lot since I was a child, and I am always surprised at how much more Westernized it becomes with each passing visit. I always feel at home with my family in Vietnam, and I look forward to every extended visit I have in my home country.

I hope you too will get a chance to visit Vietnam one day when you grow up.

---

History.com Editors. 2009. "Vietnam War." History. A&E Television Networks. October 29, 2009. history.com/topics/vietnam-war/vietnam-war-history

Gabriner, Alice. 2017. "The Vietnam War Pictures That Moved Them Most." TIME.com. TIME. 2017. time.com/vietnam-photos

Spector, Ronald H. 2019. "Vietnam War—the U.S. Role Grows." In Encyclopædia Britannica. britannica.com/event/Vietnam-War/The-U-S-role-grows

Human Rights Watch. 2020. "World Report 2021: Rights Trends in Vietnam." Human Rights Watch. December 16, 2020. www.hrw.org/world-report/2021/country-chapters/vietnam

"Vietnam." United States Department of State. state.gov/reports/2021-country-reports-on-human-rights-practices/vietnam/

"The Vietnam War | PBS." pbs.org/show/vietnam-war

# ACKNOWLEDGMENTS

This book was incredibly hard to write, and I nearly gave up on it multiple times. I wrote the first pages of this novel in 2016 and won the SCBWI's Work-in-Progress award in the Multicultural category that same year. Then, I got writer's block in the middle and couldn't make myself write to the end. So, I decided to go to grad school for creative writing, and it was at the Vermont College of Fine Arts that I finished the first draft of this novel. It has gone through many, many revisions since then, and I am so thankful and grateful to see it finally published.

I'm so thankful to my friends and family who have supported me along my writing journey. I am especially grateful to my American grandmother, Miss Helen, who taught me how to read after I came to America as a little girl, and Pat White, my American "dad," who spent hours reading books to my sister and me. He fostered my love of reading and literature, and I am so grateful to him. I'm quite sad that they didn't live to see my first publication. I miss them every day.

Thank you to my parents, Hoang and Mỹ Dung, for their sacrifices through the years. Raising children in a completely different culture is hard, and I was a difficult child. I wanted nothing to do with my Vietnamese culture and heritage as a teenager—I felt that my parents were shoving it down my throat—but now I embrace it and love my roots. I believe you must cherish where you came from to know who you are and who you are to become. I've visited Vietnam many times as an adult, and when I go back, I feel completely at home.

All my love to my husband, Joshua Patalano, who read too many versions of this book to count. Thank you for your unconditional love and support. Lots of love to my son, Luke, who inspires me to keep my heritage alive, so that I can pass it on to him.

To my agent, Sara Megibow, thank you a million times over for believing in this book and finding it the perfect home. Many thanks to my wonderful editor, Elise McMullen-Ciotti, who has fought hard for this story and helped shape it into something amazing. I am so appreciative of your guidance and editorial feedback.

I am thankful to Shellie Brauener and Wendy Brotherlin for your wisdom and feedback on the early pages of this novel. To my VCFA besties, Jessica Guerrasio and Gail Vannelli, who have been so encouraging as I faced rejection after rejection in my publication journey, thanks for always believing in me, and for your kindness and encouragement when I needed it most. Special thanks to my VCFA advisors: Sharon Darrow, who helped push me to finish the first draft of this novel; Tom Birdseye, who taught me how to become a better plotter; Shelley Tanaka for her thorough edits; and Martha Brockenbrough for always believing in me!

To my good friend Joshua Bruce, thank you for reading countless versions of this novel and for your unwavering support through the years. Thank you for never letting me give up even when I wanted to.

Finally, a big thank you to my best friend, Emily Ould, for reading all my books and offering such helpful advice and feedback. You are always there when I need you, and I'm so thankful to have met you!

# ABOUT THE AUTHOR

Đoan Phương Nguyen was born in Vietnam and immigrated to the United States in elementary school. She's always wanted to be a writer, ever since she was a little girl. Despite her parents wishing she would become a doctor or an engineer, she continued to write poems and  stories and was determined to become a children's book author. She is a graduate of Vanderbilt University, and she earned her MFA in Writing for Children & Young Adults at the Vermont College of Fine Arts (VCFA). When she's not writing, she's a photographer. She's happily married and is the parent of the cutest Vietnamese American son.

# RESOURCES FOR EDUCATORS

Visit our website, leeandlow.com, for a complete Teacher's Guide for *Mèo and Bé* as well as discussion questions, author interviews, and more!

Use your phone to scan the **QR CODE** below:

Our **Teacher's Guides** are developed by professional educators and offer extensive teaching ideas, curricular connections, and activities that can be adapted to many different educational settings.

### How Lee & Low Books Supports Educators:

Lee & Low Books is the largest children's book publisher in the country focused exclusively on diverse books. We publish award-winning books for beginning readers through young adults, along with free, high-quality educational resources to support our titles.

Browse our website to discover Teacher's Guides for 600+ books along with book trailers, interviews, and more.

We are honored to support educators in preparing the next generation of readers, thinkers, and global citizens.

**LEE & LOW BOOKS**
ABOUT EVERYONE • FOR EVERYONE